The Second I Do

ELLE DE'VON

To all the Black Women who still believe in love!

Synopsis

Harper Moore had her dream wedding all planned—right down to the last rose petal. But when she wakes up in Las Vegas with a ring on her finger and the wrong man in her bed, her carefully curated world spins out of control. The man she accidentally married, Xavier Pierce is charming, unapologetic, and the last person she ever expected to call her husband.

Given three weeks to prepare for a new life and break the news to her high-profile fiancé, Harper scrambles to undo the biggest mistake of her life. But the longer she stays married to Xavier, the harder it becomes to convince herself it *was* a mistake. Between the heat of their chemistry and the truths that begin to surface, Harper starts to question everything she thought she wanted.

As secrets unravel and loyalties are tested, Harper is

forced to confront the woman she's become and the one she's always been too afraid to be. In the chaos of her so-called mistake, she may just discover that saying *I do* to Xavier Pierce was the best decision she's ever made.

CHAPTER ONE

What Happens in Vegas

The wheels hit the tarmac, and I hoped that Vegas was everything that I needed and more. After I deboard the plane, I found the *Bride Tribe* waiting for me at baggage claim since I was the last one to arrive. I was extra annoyed after Karter said we were going to the cake tasting before I left for my bachelorette trip. I thought I had planned the cake tasting for next week, but maybe I had mixed it up .

Trying to shake off the agitation of almost missing my flight because Karter couldn't decide on a flavor, I was determined to put all of that behind me and have the best time. When we got into the waiting limo, Summer was the first to pop the bottles. They passed the glasses around before she poured everyone a glass.

"My bitch is getting marrieeeeeddddddd!" Summer

said holding up her glass. We all screamed and toasted to the sentiment, but deep down, I wasn't even sure if I still wanted to do this. We pulled onto the strip, and Vegas was alive. Music thumped through the lobby of the hotel, becoming the soundtrack to laughter spilling down the hallway, the sea of sequins and stilettos scattered like confetti.

After getting checked in, I went to my room to get dressed and ready for the night. I had paired a silver cocktail dress with my black fuck me pumps. Karter had already texted me four times since I had been out of the shower, and I was over his shit.

> Karter: Have you landed yet?
>
> Karter: You need to check in.
>
> Karter: Are you ignoring me?
>
> Karter: Be an adult and send me an update once you're settled.

I felt like he was trying to suffocate me, and for once, I just wanted to breathe. I walked over to the bar and took a shot of Patron to start the night right. If this was my last night with my girls, I was going to make it worth it.

I checked my phone to find out where we were

meeting, since the girls had already been pregaming before I arrived. Harley sent the details of where to find them in the group chat

Harley: We are downstairs Blue's Lounge, first booth near the back.

So I went down to meet them there. My friends were already halfway through their second bottle of champagne, arguing about who had the best dress. Harley, of course, was winning, wearing a silky red dress that hugged her body. She looked like the poster child for sin.

When they saw me walk up they all shrieked with excitement like they had forgotten I was the reason for the trip. I sat with them, looking around out of habit. Over the past few months, there have been times when I was out with my girls and Karter would just show up. It had become an expectation at this point.

"Harper, you look too sexy to be acting nervous," Harley said, hands on her hips. "This is your *bachelorette*, not a church revival."

"I'm just tired." I tried to laugh.

"You're always tired." She rolled her eyes. "You've been planning that wedding like it's the Olympics."

"It feels like it."

She poured another drink and handed it to me. "Then tonight, you retire. You drink. You dance. You forget about Karter for one damn night."

Forget Karter? Was that even possible at this point? He was woven into every fiber of my life, so forgetting him felt impossible.

He'd texted earlier:

> Karter: Be safe. Remember, image matters. No wild photos.

I'd stared at the message for a long time, wondering when *I love you* had been replaced by *image matters*.

I decided to take Harley's advice and let my hair down. Fuck it. If this was going to be my last night of freedom, I was going to embrace it with open arms.

"Let the liquor rain!" I said, throwing back the drink and three shots sitting on the table.

The club was a blur of lights and laughter. Everywhere smelled like perfume, money, and temptation. The DJ was killing it, bass vibrating in my chest causing my hips to involuntarily move. Harley caught my movement and dragged me to the dance floor. The beat caught me, and I danced like tomorrow was never going to show up. I could feel the heat pouring over my body, but I didn't know where it was coming from.

That's when I saw him. Across the room, near the bar. Fuck he was fine. Tall, skin smooth like melted bronze, smile lazy, wearing a black button-down rolled at the sleeves, a watch glinting against his wrist.

At first, I looked around to see where he was staring because he surely wasn't looking at me like this. But he wasn't looking around like everyone else. He was *looking*. At me. Like I was the last drop of water on a hot day in Florida.

I looked away, pretending to laugh at something Harley said, but my curiosity was louder than the caution Karter had given. When I looked back, he was gone.

Hours later, the party had moved upstairs to a private lounge. It was decked out in gold and velvet, reeking of bad decisions waiting to happen. Someone ordered another round. The girls were loud, posing for photos. I knew that I couldn't be seen looking unkept, so I opted out of the taking photos with the girls.

While they laughed and snapped photos for social media, I sat on the edge of the couch across the room, heels dangling, drink sweating, begging to be drank in my hand. Watching them have the time of their lives while I contemplated my own.

I smelled him before I heard the voice slide in beside me.

"Looks like you could use a real toast."

I turned, and there he was, wearing the same smile, but his scent made him that much more dangerous. When I looked up, he was closer now. The smell of bourbon and clean skin mixed with something tantalizing. His eyes were the color of old whiskey, and I knew if I stared into them too long, I would be in trouble.

"Do I know you?" I asked.

"Not yet," he said, smiling. "But we can fix that."

I laughed louder than I meant to. "You always this confident?"

"Only when it works."

He lifted his glass. "To the woman who looks like she's deciding between staying put or running for her life."

"What makes you think I'm running?" I stared at him.

He shrugged. "The way you keep checking the door."

I didn't realize I was. I guess not even alcohol could make me forget my habits.

"Why are you over here alone?" he asked.

"Now I know you see all those giggling heathens over there." I nodded over to where the crew was still taking pictures and dancing seductively for reels.

"Why are you not having fun with them? From their reaction earlier, isn't this supposed to be for you?" He smiled, showing his white teeth and the glint of the diamonds in his bottom grill.

"What makes you think I'm not having fun?" I wasn't about to tell this stranger that the optics would look bad on my fiancé if I were caught in any of those videos.

"Look at them, then look at you." He pointed to my friends and then to the mirror in front of us. And damn if he wasn't right. I looked like money, but there was a glimmer of something in my eyes I couldn't put my finger on.

"You know what, you're right. Fuck this shit." I pulled the pin out of my bun and let my hair down.

He held out a hand, and I almost said no. I almost remembered Karter's text, my mother's voice, my own habit of saying *I'm fine*. Instead, I took it.

I stood and straightened my dress, and as soon as he interlaced his fingers in mine, the music changed. It was slow and bass-heavy, as if we were the reason for it. His hand found the small of my back, and I felt it everywhere.

He leaned close, his breath warm against my ear. "You don't belong in a box, Harper."

My head snapped up. "How do you know my name?"

He smiled. "Your friend yelled it across the room earlier."

"You're smooth." I laughed, exhaling the tension that was building.

"I like to think I'm observant."

"Those are not the same thing."

"Maybe not," he said. "But both'll get me a second dance."

He was right, we danced until the crowd blurred. The world around us shrank to heat, music, and the sound of our laughter.

At some point, Harley appeared, with her camera flashing. "Okay, mystery man! Don't steal my sister before the wedding!"

He winked at her. "No promises."

Later, there were shots I didn't remember ordering, stories from my girls I didn't remember happening, and laughter I didn't know still belonged to me.

Then flashes of the elevator doors, gold numbers blinking, his hand steady at my waist. The scent of cologne, the taste of bourbon, and something sweet. Him. Unlike Karter, his kiss didn't feel like a mistake.

"Tell me your name again," I whispered as the suite door closed behind us.

"Xion Pierce," he said. "Nice to meet you again."

The rest of the night disappeared into laughter and vibes.

CHAPTER TWO

It's Morning

I woke up with the kind of headache that felt like somebody was playing spades with my brain and reneging on purpose.

The room was too bright, the air too cold, and something familiar. An expensive cologne layered over last night's champagne, with a hint of cocoa butter and trouble. My lashes fluttered against the satin pillowcase, and I did that thing where you breathe slow like you can fool a hangover into thinking you're still asleep.

I tried to roll over and realized my fingertips brushed a chest.

A very warm, very chiseled, very *not*-Karter chest.

My eyes flew open so fast my pupils protested. I was in a suite with floor-to-ceiling windows, with the Vegas skyline strutting like she owned the place, gold accents everywhere. Looking around, I saw my red-bottomed heels discarded near the door, and my dress was draped over a chair. There was a satin bonnet on my head, and surprisingly, I wasn't naked. I looked under the cover to find I was wearing a black satin pajama set with Mrs. P embossed on the sleeve.

Who the hell was Mrs. P, and why was I wearing her fucking pajamas?

But the biggest elephant in the room, was the man in my bed!

His brown skin with caramel undertones kissed by the sun. Fresh fade, waves tight enough to make any boat rock, a full mouth, and a beard lined so crisp it could cut you. He was sprawled on his back, sheet hitched low on perfect hips, not hiding the nice-sized bulge peeking beneath it.

For a second, I began to panic. Sitting up too fast, and the room tilted. My hand flew to my head, but something else caught my eye, causing me to freeze. I pulled my hand back down, looking at the ring.

The ring on my finger wasn't mine.

Mine was a cushion-cut halo Karter picked because it photographed well, a compromise between my taste and what he said "looked right with the brand." (Yes, my life had a brand. Corporate fiancé, corporate ring.) This ring gleamed differently: a clean, emerald-cut diamond in a cathedral setting, elegant and unapologetic, like it had nothing to prove. Like whoever put it there had known exactly what I wanted before I admitted it.

My stomach dropped to somewhere between the mattress and the Persian rug.

"Good morning, Mrs. Pierce!" My whole world stopped!

The voice came lazy and velvet-warm, with a Southern drawl that slid up my spine. He rolled onto his side, propping his head on his hand, and smiled at me like I was the sunrise he'd been praying for.

"Who are you?" The words came out dry and raspy, due to what I could only assume was dehydration.

He chuckled. "Xion. We covered that about—" He pretended to count on his fingers. "—six times last night."

I clutched the sheet to my chest like modesty decided to clock in late. "I'm engaged."

He glanced at my left hand pointedly. "You were last night. But today you're married."

"I—no." My voice wobbled. "No, no. That's not—I didn't marry anyone."

"You're right, you didn't marry anyone. You married me!" He sat up, unbothered, sexy as hell, and I hated him a little for it. He leaned in, tapped the new ring with his thumb. "Also, you're welcome."

"For what?" I snapped, too soft to land properly.

"For being one of the best things to happen to you in a long time. I think that's how you worded it." He grinned, then softened. "Relax, Harper. Breathe."

My name in his mouth pressed every nerve I had left. "We didn't—how did—" I squeezed my eyes shut and caught only flashes: a private lounge with a baseline you could feel in your bones; a cigar that wasn't mine but tasted like laughter; his hand at the small of my back; the way he'd said my name like prayer, not possession. I remembered the heat of his gaze, then saying yes to something that finally felt like mine.

My phone lit up on the nightstand, face-down, buzzing like my guilty conscience. I flipped it over to find the group chat—*Bride Tribe* 💍—was going off. I didn't look at any of the messages because I knew I wasn't ready for whatever Harley had to say about last night.

Harley was not only my sister, but my maid of honor. Since we were little, she was my other half. When our mother insisted we share everything, we didn't mind because we already did. She had planned this trip with Leesa and Summer—three days of poolside pictures, a pole class for laughs, one "classy" club night where everyone promised we'd be in bed by two like responsible adults.

It was nine-fifteen on day two, and I was in bed. The wrong bed. Married. To the wrong man.

I swallowed. "This is... a misunderstanding."

"Probably," Xion agreed easily. "And we can misunderstand each other later."

He swung those long legs off the mattress and stood to stretch, giving me an eyeful of the Lord's good work! He reached for a pair of grey sweats, dragged them up over hips God had taken his time on, then padded to the kitchenette like he lived here.

I stared at the ring again. My heart was thudding hard enough to shake answers loose. I had a fiancé back in Chicago who liked his shirts ironed a certain way, and audited my Instagram captions like they were presentations, and I was sitting here with blurred memories and a husband.

Karter and I've been together for five years. He'd proposed to me in front of his coworkers at a rooftop party "spontaneously," which I later learned meant he'd scheduled the photographer two weeks in advance. He said we were perfect together, and the next step was a promotion to fiancé.

Xion returned with two glasses of water and slid one into my hand. His fingers were warm with calluses that had been cared for, like a man who signed contracts and still knew how to carry furniture. He sat on the edge of the bed, close enough for my breath to remember his.

"What happened?" I asked, hoping that he could give me clarity.

"We met," he said. "You said you were tired of being reasonable. I said I'd be all the reason you would ever need."

"That sounds like me," I muttered, horrified that I had said these things to a stranger.

He proceeded to fill in the gaps of what I could remember. He was patient with me, never once getting frustrated with the millions of questions I would ask after he told me a detail I didn't remember.

"You danced with your eyes closed." He smiled as if he were unlocking a core memory. "You laughed until your sides were sore. And when the night finally got quiet, you told me your secrets like you needed to escape them."

"Secrets, what secrets?" I wondered praying that I hadn't embarrassed myself too bad.

"You hate your wedding playlist." I exhaled hoping that nothing else was too bad.

"Karter curated it." I said, relieved.

"Of course he did." Xion's mouth twitched. "You want Erykah and Mary. He picked Ed Sheeran twice."

"You also told me how you felt like you're trapped,

how he has treated this relationship transactionally as if marriage is strictly for show." I covered my face. How could I share such things with him when I didn't even say them to my therapist.

I groaned into my water. "Please tell me we didn't…"

"Don't insult me like that. There would be no questions if we had!" My legs clenched at the authority in his tone.

"We didn't do anything crazy outside of getting married. I would like my wife to remember our wedding night." He said, brows furrowed.

He reached into the drawer of the nightstand and handed me a folded piece of paper. It was a marriage certificate with our signatures and a smear of glitter. There was a Polaroid attached, of us at the altar with Elvis and the bartender from the bar. I recognized my handwriting immediately.

"This is insane." I rubbed my temples trying to message in the truth of what I had done.

"Mmm." He tipped his head, studying me. "Or it's the first sane decision you made in a while."

"Don't do that," I snapped. "Just because you caught me at a vulnerable time, and married me doesn't mean you know anything about me."

He snorted and took the insult on the chin. "I know

you felt so trapped that you were willing to marry a stranger in Vegas so you didn't have to marry the man you don't even want as your fiancé." His words cut deep but softened as he continued. "I also know you don't like eggs unless they're scrambled soft with cheese, and you apologize when you disagree like you're not allowed to have your own opinion. I also know you look good in the morning, even when you're mad at me."

"Not a high bar." I said trying to act like this man wasn't reading me for filth right now.

"High enough, that you married me in less than 12 hours ago," he said, unbothered.

He rubbed his temples then he stopped abruptly, as if remembering something inconvenient, he glanced at my ring again. He looked back at me and smiled.

"You have three weeks." The look in his eyes were serious and I knew he was serious but that didn't stop me from asking.

"Are you for real right now?" I tilted my head to the side like he was crazy.

"In three weeks, I'm coming to Chicago. And my wife is coming home with me." He said it like it was a fact.

"You can pack light or heavy. That part's your business. But when I pull up, know that I'm not leaving without you."

My mouth fell open. "Excuse me?"

"Three weeks, Harper." He stood, leaned down quickly, and kissed my temple, causing a spike in my blood pressure.

"Are you—are you threatening me?" My voice lifted like it had somewhere to be.

"Promising you." His eyes softened. "It's time to leave this life behind but I'm only giving you three weeks to get your affairs in order.

A knock rattled the suite door. I jumped so hard I sloshed water on my thigh. Xion chuckled and slid his hands in his pockets and went to answer it, opening the door only a crack.

"Housekeeping," a woman's voice sang, she had a familiar accent and was overly cheerful. "Check out is at eleven, baby. You need more towels?"

"We're good," he said, smoothly. He closed the door and turned, that easy smile dimming as he took me in.

"I have some other business to tend to today so I'm going to go shower." He grabbed a towel, and paused. "You can call your people. Or not. Your decision, Mrs. Pierce."

He disappeared into the bathroom, and the shower hissed to life. I stared at the certificate again until the words went fuzzy. My phone buzzed three times in a row, then a Face-Time ring vibrated through the wood of the nightstand. Karter's contact picture bounced around the screen. My stomach clenched as I thought about everything.

Instead of answering, I declined the call and opened the *Bride Tribe* chat.

> Harley: You up, sis? Brunch at 10? I'm starving !

> Summer: U good? U went ghost last night

> Leesa: Where you at?

> Harley: Harper? Babe answer.

I typed, then deleted, and tried to type again, but what could I say? My hands shook as I held the phone. How much did they know? Where were they when I was getting married? Why did they allow me to leave with a strange man? My mind was racing and I felt like I was suffocating. But something in me, the small voice I'd learned to hush and wait for the freudian slip, said *just wait.*

The bathroom door opened with a burst of steam, reminding me that I was not alone. Xion emerged in fresh sweats and a white tee that took clung to his biceps for dear life. He had a chain at his throat, simple and gold, and a gold ring on his left ring finger. His outfit was simple, but you could tell he was a man who moved with intention. He eyed the phone in my hand.

"You going to answer that?" Karter was calling for the third time and I was about to lose it.

"I don't know what to tell him." I exhaled, a laugh without humor. "Hey, babe, funny story. Turns out I auditioned for a new life and got the part?" I rolled my eyes. He was really working my last nerve.

"Tell him your true feelings and you think you shouldn't get married. In that order. Let me deal with the rest."

"And how are you going to deal with it?" I looked up sharply.

"Three weeks," he said, no hesitation. "And after that, whatever you don't handle, I will."

"You're very sure of yourself."

"I'm very sure of *you*." He nodded toward the window, toward the city glittering like a dare.

"The woman I met last night didn't belong to anybody but herself, and she was dope as fuck. I think you would like her. I'm trying to have her around all the time, she deserves that."

My throat tightened. I pulled my knees up to my chest, hugging them, the ring flashing in the light.

"This shit is ridiculous." I say closing my eyes trying to wish myself awake from this dream.

"Sometimes ridiculous is how freedom shows up. She's beautiful and loud so you can't pretend you didn't hear her, wearing a silver dress and black Red bottoms."

"Do you practice these lines in the mirror?"

"I was raised by a Black woman who told me not to waste words. So when I want something, I say it plain." He laughed, soft and genuine.

"And what do you want?"

"You, Harper. But not this you. The one from last night, that was honest, unmanaged and happy."He didn't miss a beat telling me what he wanted.

"Don't...don't make promises you'll regret." I swallowed hard peeking up at him as I still clutched my knees.

"I don't do regret," he said.

Then he pulled my hand from around my legs and I let him. Holding my hand he leaned down and pressed a kiss to the back of my hand, right over the ring that didn't lie. His mouth lingered there, respectful and certain.

"Three weeks, Mrs. Pierce." He slipped a card onto the nightstand. I looked over to see his name, number, an address in Atlanta that sounded like money and high maintenance, before heading for the door.

"Xion?"

He paused, turning. "Yeah, Mrs. Pierce?"

I hated how good that sounded rolling off his lips.

"What if I don't come?"

He smiled, not cocky but sincere and patient, like a man who could wait out a storm.

"Then dinner with Karter is going to be really weird with me sitting at the head of the table."

The door clicked behind him and silence rushed in, bringing the breath back into my lungs this man had just stolen. I stared at the simple elegance of the ring, the certificate tying me to a man who was determined to make me his. But the flashes of the version of myself who had danced with her eyes closed made me miss who I used to be. My phone vibrated again, and I instantly grew annoyed to see Karters face flashing on the screen.

I tossed it on the bed and let it ring.

My phone buzzed again with a text from an unknown number.

Unknown: Tick Tock!

CHAPTER THREE

The Wrong Ring

Walking over to the window, the warmth of the sun on my skin helped to calm me a little. Standing in the light felt good in the moment. It didn't care about my confusion, my marital status, or the fact that my stomach was somewhere between hunger and guilt.

The knock at the door pulled me back to reality.

"For you, Mrs. Pierce. Your husband sent these from the boutiques in the hotel. Enjoy!" The bellhop said bringing in four bags from designer stores located in the hotel.

"Thank you," I say, taking the bags from his hands.

My phone buzzed again, and I knew I had to start getting ready. I stood in front of the mirror, pressing a cool cloth to my face. The woman looking back at me had yesterday's lashes hanging on for dear life, and that damn ring was still sparkling like it belonged on my finger. I decided to shower and see if that would make me feel better. Getting out, I looked over at the bags curiously.

I peeked inside and found makeup, a golden Cartier bracelet, and an outfit with a note on top.

Dear Mrs. Pierce,

I hope you enjoy the gift. Now go enjoy the rest of your trip.

-X.

I stood there, baffled, holding the black card that had fallen out of the note. I looked at his name embossed in matte black on the card. Was he serious?

"Okay, Harper. You can do this." I whispered to myself. "Smile, you're just going to brunch. Act normal."

I slipped on the ivory jumpsuit with the matching sandals. Pulled my curls into a high puff and headed downstairs to the hotel restaurant where the *Bride Tribe* was holding court.

I heard Harley before I saw her, laughing too loudly at something Summer said. She looked perfect, as usual, skin glowing, edges crisp, her locs twisted into a crown like a goddess. She shrieked when she spotted me and began to wave frantically as if she could be missed.

"There's the bride!" she sang, like she hadn't left me with a stranger to end up married last night.

"Literally!" I muttered, sliding into the reserved chair between Leesa and Summer.

I hugged and air-kissed Harley before leaning in and hugging Summer, while Leesa flagged down the server.

"Mimosas for the table, please. Heavy on the champagne—our girl's getting married!" I almost choked on air.

Harley smirked. "She better, Karter would have a stroke if you called it off this close to the wedding."

"Yeah..." I picked at my napkin.

If only I were that lucky.

Summer cut in, stopping me from saying what I was thinking.

"Speaking of Satan. Girl, why did he text me at five a.m. asking if I'd seen you? I waited to respond because who the hell does he think he is, texting me at that time of morning, demanding answers? But when I did respond, I told him to get those tighty whities out of his ass. And that you are sleeping like sane people are at that time of fucking morning."

"Appreciate it," I said, forcing a smile.

The mimosas arrived, and the sight of them made my head hurt all over again. Harley handed me mine and clinked our glasses.

"To Harper, the last single brunch before she becomes Mrs. Peoples!"

"I still can't believe you are changing your name to that shit." Summer chimed in before taking a huge gulp.

The table erupted in laughter. I sipped my mimosa, trying to wrap my mind around everything. The ring on my finger caught the light, and Harley spat mimosa all over the table.

"Ohhhhh shit. You got a new ring? I didn't see that last night," she said. "Did Karter upgrade you?"

My throat went dry. "Uh, no. This one is fake. I didn't want anything to happen to mine while we were here, so I put it in the safe."

"Well bitch send me the link to that because that bitch sparkles like the real deal!" Leesa raised a brow.

"It's comfortable," I lied, sliding my hand under the table.

"That's smart, because we are about to get into some shit!" Harley's gaze lingered on the ring.

"Just trying to keep the real thing safe. Vegas is a hell of a place." I answered too quickly, so I didn't seem suspicious.

Summer snorted. "Shit, may as well get married while you're here too." The laughter that followed was light, but Harley's wasn't. Hers was tight around the edges, like she knew something I didn't.

"So," Leesa said, changing the subject, "what's the plan for today? Pool? Spa? Apology texts?"

"Spa," I said without a second thought. "Definitely the spa."

Harley leaned forward, her tone turning syrupy. "You okay, Harp? You look...off."

"I'm good." My insides felt like they were ready to crawl up my throat.

"Karter said you two had a little argument before the trip. Something about your guest list?" Harley could be so messy at times, and I hated it, but what pissed me off more was how Karter was filling her in on our shit when he was the one who had an issue with her having a plus one to the wedding.

I blinked. "He told you we argued about the guest list?"

"Yeah, he's worried about you sis." She shrugged, sipping the rest of her mimosa.

That word, worried, landed wrong. Karter's name didn't even belong in the same sentence as the human emotion worry. Karter managed. Hell, he micromanaged emotions.

"More like he's worried about you." The words tumbled out before I could catch them.

"What the hell does that even mean?" Summer asked, chiming in on the conversation.

I exhaled.

"After the cake tasting, Karter decided that we needed to revisit the guest list. He told me that Harley didn't need to have a plus one because she never brings her boy toys around anyway, and we could use the spot somewhere else." Leesa didn't say a word, but I caught the pointed look she gave Harley. It was like she knew something but wasn't saying it.

"The fuck." Summer spoke, breaking my spiral.

"I know, right. Then, when I asked him who else would be coming alone who needed the seat, he said he needed to think about it. So, I told him he was just trying to control things as usual, and if my sister wanted to bring her fucking vibrator, she could!" I thought they would have laughed or even high-fived me for standing up for myself, but instead, everyone was silent.

"Anyway," Harley said, brushing it off, "he loves you, Harper. Don't overthink it. You two are perfect together."

Perfect huh? That's hilarious.

Leesa rolled her eyes and shook her head. I wondered what all that was about but decided not to ask right now. I would talk to her later today when everyone wasn't around.

I reached for my phone to escape the moment. A text popped up from an unsaved number. I knew who it was from the first message. Against my better judgment, I decided to save the number.

> Xion: Have you made it to brunch yet?
>
> Xion: Don't order eggs without cheese.
>
> Xion: You'll just be mad.
>
> Xion: You look gorgeous when you're flustered. And I knew that Ivory would look amazing against your skin.

I nearly dropped the phone.

"Who's that?" Harley asked. She caught the shift in

my demeanor and used it to steer the conversation away from her. Typical.

"Work," I answered almost too quickly.

"But you don't work weekends." I wasn't sure if she was suspicious or if I was being paranoid at this point.

"It's the planning reminders, I have set up as emails," I said, shoving the phone away.

"Girl, are you planning a whole new life?" Summer laughed.

"Definitely feels that way!" I sighed.

The waiter returned with pancakes and shrimp & grits, accompanied by a small plate of eggs with cheese I didn't order. I instantly got butterflies, but my stomach betrayed me with a growl. As I ate, conversation swirled around weddings, spa packages, and Karter's supposed "romantic streak." I tuned them out, the sound fading behind a new memory trying to surface.

A dance floor. Gold lights. Xion's hand on my back. His voice in my ear: *You sure this is the life you want?*

Harley's laugh snapped me back. "So, Harper, tell the truth, any cold feet?"

"Something like that." I looked at her dead in the eye, causing her to look away.

Her smile faltered. Just for a second, but I saw it. She recovered quickly by toasting again.

"To the bride who always lands on her feet." Everyone at the table cheered, causing the other tables around us to join in.

By the time brunch ended, my head was pounding again. "Don't let Vegas make you stupid, okay? Karter loves you, so go put some slippers on those cold feet."

Her perfume was familiar and too sweet. I knew I had smelled it before, but I couldn't place it in the moment.

As I walked out of the restaurant to go to my room, my phone buzzed again.

Xion: 20 days, Mrs. Pierce.

I stared at the message, then at the city glittering beyond the glass doors. Twenty days. And somehow, that didn't sound like a threat. It sounded like a countdown to freedom.

When I got to my room, my key didn't work, so I had to head back down to the front desk.

"Good afternoon, how can I help you with your stay?" The concierge asked as I approached.

"Good afternoon. My room key is not working."

"Oh no, let's get that fixed for you. May I have your name and room number, please?"

"Harper Moore. And the room is five thirty-four in the West tower." She smiled and began to type.

"Um. I'm sorry. Could the name be under a different last name?" She asked apologetically.

"I am here for my bachelorette party, so maybe. But I could have sworn when I checked in yesterday, it was under Moore.

"Ah, okay. Let me look in one other place." I waited patiently as she pressed the keys.

"There you are. I see what the problem is now." She smiled as she gave me another room key and signaled the bellhop.

"It looks like your husband upgraded your room to the North Tower with a penthouse suite. Your things have already been moved from your old room, but he also had some other packages delivered here for you while you were out at brunch. So, I am going to have your personal concierge, Michael, take you up to your suite. Your Butler Alexander is there awaiting your arrival." I stood there in shock. There was no way Karter had done all of this because of an argument. I pulled out my phone to text him on the way up to the room.

Thank you so much. This is shaping up to be the best trip yet.

I smiled and danced a little.

"I'm so happy we could be the reason for your smile. Enjoy the rest of your stay, Mrs. Pierce." My head snapped back around so fast I was sure to have a concussion later.

"What?" I said, looking at her.

"Oh, I'm sorry, do you prefer to be called Ms. Moore until after we get the official marriage license back?" The room blurred.

"Marriage License?" I managed to stammer out.

"Yes, Mr. Pierce had us put a rush on the marriage license that you signed, and it looks like you should have your certificate before you check out. Is that still okay?" I stared at her blankly.

"It's fine, checkout is fine. I'm sorry you caught me off guard with the name. Guess I'm not used to hearing that title yet. It has a ring to it, though." I said, showing her the ring Xion picked, hoping to distract her from how flustered I was at the moment.

"Girl, he's a keeper." She gasped and snapped her fingers.

I smiled, turning to follow Michael up to my new room. The room had to be exclusive because there was a private elevator, and he showed me how to use my key to get upstairs to my room. I had only seen things like this in movies. Part of me felt like I wasn't supposed to be accepting any of this treatment, like I should have been trying to figure out how to get out of this. But there was a piece of me that wanted to walk on the wild side for once and choose myself.

Harper, you're in Vegas. Live in the moment and worry about the rest later.

The private elevator opened into a world of glass and temptation. Floor-to-ceiling windows framed the glittering Vegas Strip, its neon pulse flickering across marble floors and velvet furniture. A grand piano sat untouched near the window, and a crystal chandelier dripped light over the room.

Beyond the living space, the bedroom waited, hosting dark suede comforters, white linen, and a view that could make anyone forget their sins. The bathroom was pure indulgence, with a glass-and-stone shower, a steam room, and a tub large enough for two.

A discreet knock announced the butler, gloved and silent, carrying champagne already chilled. In this penthouse, luxury wasn't a thing; it was a feeling, one you could taste in every breath.

"Thank you.. Alexander?" I hesitated to take a sip of the drink.

"Yes, Mrs. Pierce. I am Alexandor. I will be your butler for the duration of your stay here at the Grand Tower." His voice was smooth and heavily accented. I couldn't place the accent, but I knew if I didn't ask, it was going to plague me.

"Nice to meet you, Alexander. May I ask where you are from?" He smiled, as if he appreciated my asking instead of guessing.

"Ma'am, I am Peruvian." My eyes lit up.

His accent reminded me of the senior trip we took to Peru in High School. That was almost ten years ago, but I never forgot the accent.

I wanted to tell him about my trip to Peru, but he had lived there his whole life, so there was no need for me to share my view of his home country. Instead, I extended my hand to him as a greeting, setting the tone for our time together during my stay.

Just as I was about to start up another conversation with Alexandor, my phone buzzed. I pulled it out and saw Karter's face bouncing around the screen. Knowing that I couldn't avoid him the entire trip, I excused myself and wandered out to the balcony in the bedroom.

The call connected, and I instantly regretted answering. Karter had the phone propped up on his desk, scowling.

"I hope you're having fun on this little... Trip." He said, expressions not changing.

"Hello, to you too, Karter," I say, not allowing him to pull me into his energy.

"Oh, I'm sorry. Me not speaking is an issue? I thought that's what you wanted since you've not answered any of my calls or texts." I rolled my eyes because Karter was ready to be dramatic, and I wasn't in the mood for the mental Gymnastics.

"Look, Karter. We agreed that I would be here in Vegas on my best behavior, and you would allow me to breathe." He tried to speak, but I continued. "I haven't been gone for twenty-four hours, and you have done everything but send out a search party to find me, and that is not okay.

"Harper, you need to be reasonable." He said, leaning forward, looking a bit shocked.

"No, Karter, I don't. This is my bachelorette weekend, and I am going to enjoy it. And you are going to let me. Now I will see you in two days. Surely you can make it that long without me." He smirked, and I knew I would pay for this later.

"Okay, Harper. Enjoy your girls' trip with Leesa, Summer, and Harley. I will see you when you get home!" He ended the call, and I smiled.

"Did that feel good?" Xion said, voice cutting into my celebratory moment.

"Jinkee's. You scared me." I shrieked.

Xion burst out laughing. "Did you just say.. Never mind." He walked over to where I was standing, and I could feel the butterflies in my stomach take flight.

"What on earth are you doing here? I know you don't think you are staying here with me." He smirked.

"Harper, as bad as I want to stay here and get to know my wife more, I can't. My business here is finished, and I need to get back home. I just wanted to see you before I left."

"Well, you've seen me," I said, spinning so he could see my whole body.

"Cute. I'm going to head out now. But remember what I said. Twenty Days, then I step in!" He stepped in and kissed my lips gently like he owned them. It felt so right that I couldn't even pull away, and when he did, I instantly missed the warmth of his lips on mine.

What is wrong with you, Harper? This is not your husband.

No matter how many times I told myself that, my body never listened.

I turned to look out at the city as his footsteps faded into the distance. Taking a deep breath, I decided to embrace this trip and have the time of my life because soon I would be caged forever.

CHAPTER FOUR

Tick-Tock

By the time I landed back in Chicago, the whole trip felt like a fever dream. We danced, sang, laughed, and partied like it was 1999, literally. We had a '90s-themed party bus that took us to all the hottest clubs. I danced with the strippers and drank with a drunk on the strip. Vegas truly didn't owe me a damn thing, except a wedding ring.

The flight home was eerily quiet, but my mind wasn't. I sat there with my phone on airplane mode, staring at the wedding Pinterest boards, taunting me from saved folders like ghosts. My hands kept drifting to the place Xion's ring had sat all weekend. I'd shoved it into my carry-on instead of leaving it behind. I had worn the ring the entire time I was in Vegas and missed the weight. But when it came time to come home, I remembered that I had no idea where Karter's ring was.

I was packing my bag to leave when I realized that I hadn't seen my ring since we left. The thought of my missing wedding ring had me on edge. I wrote in the group chat, commissioning them for support.

Me: Y'all, I can't find my wedding ring.

Summer: WHAT?

Leesa: Might be a sign.

Summer: LOL! Not a sign! I can't with you, Leesa.

Me: Can y'all be serious for 5 minutes? God, he is going to kill me.

Summer: Well then, he would be in hell because we would kill him!

Harley: Didn't you say that you left it in the safe? Maybe you should have them check the safe in the other room.

I knew that lie was going to come back and bite me in the ass. The girls had learned about my room upgrade when they came to drag me out to the party, only to find the room occupied by someone else. When they called to find out where I was, I told them the hotel had upgraded me, and they lost their minds. They even stayed the night with me. The Alaskan king bed in the room was accommodating to all of us.

> Me: Good thinking, Harley. I will go
> down and ask them.

I blew out a breath, thinking of what to do next. *Should I ask Xion if he has seen it?*

I still didn't remember everything from that night, and I was damn sure not asking Xion if he knew where the ring was.

Every time my fingers brushed the spot where *his* ring sat, a memory flickered. Us, laughing too loud, his warm touch sure of their place, and his presence bold and caring. Xion's voice was smooth like a lullaby being sung to my spirit.

Three weeks, Mrs. Pierce.

Chicago's cold hit different that evening, slapping the sense out of me and ushering in the looming feeling of panic.

By the time I pulled up to the condo, I had my mask ready: polite smile, soft tone, and all the appropriate guilt for a fiancé who got married on her bachelorette weekend. I was surprised that Karter wasn't picking me up, but after I told him to let me enjoy myself, he acted as if I had called off the wedding.

Taking my bags out of the back of the Uber, I knocked and waited. Karter opened the door before I could knock for a third time. He was wearing a crisp polo, with a fresh haircut, and a smile as rehearsed as mine.

"There she is," he said, pulling me into a hug that smelled like too much cologne and obligation. "My runaway bride."

"Hey, Karter," I murmured, stiff in his arms.

He pulled back just enough to study my face. "You didn't call me back, Harper. I gave you a chance to calm down, but you still didn't check in. You know how that looks?"

I blinked. "Like I was busy?"

"More like you were being careless." His jaw flexed. "Do you know I was worried about you?"

"Were you?" I said. I was mentally too exhausted to keep going back and forth with him.

"Are you going to let me in the house, or do I need

to go stay with my mother?" His eyes narrowed, but he covered it with a laugh.

"Oh, I'm sorry. You must be exhausted. Come in, baby."

I scoffed at him, putting my suitcase in front of me to make sure our bodies didn't touch. The last thing I needed was his cologne on my skin.

The condo looked the same, anally organized and lifeless. Our home was the kind of space that photographed well for the ideal couple-goals posts, but never felt lived in. The walls held still laughter that wasn't allowed to echo, and hugs lacking warmth. The fixture's artwork was an abstract depiction of the disorganized thoughts of my brain in this space. The candles were unscented because "strong fragrances distracted the minds." Hell, even the throw pillows had proper posture.

He took my luggage like a gentleman on autopilot. "So," he said, "Did you have fun?"

"Yeah," without offering details.

"With your phone turned off?" he scolded.

"It wasn't off. It was on Do Not Disturb. Gosh, I just needed a break, Karter." I said, exasperated.

"From what? Your life is perfect!"

From you. And perfect for who? If this is perfect, then I crave imperfection!

"From planning," I said instead. "From people. From... everything."

He observed me with that calculating silence many mistook for patience. "You know, sometimes when you disappear like that, it makes me look..."

"Bad?" I finished for him.

He smiled without warmth. "Uninformed. You didn't even tell Harley where you were half the time."

"Why would I need to tell her when she could see me? And how would you know what Harley knew? Were you using my sister to spy on me?" I laughed incredulously.

His expression shifted; something cold lay behind the charm he displayed. "She's your sister, Harper. I reached out to her since you said that you wanted to enjoy your time in Vegas."

"If you were going to do all of this just to keep tabs on me, you should have just popped up like you always do any other time!" I snapped.

"If it weren't so far away, I would have. But I had pressing matters here and couldn't get away! Besides, I don't have time to keep babysitting you. At some point, you have to grow up, Harper!" I inhaled, trying to calm my nerves because he really just admitted to following me.

I rolled my eyes, knowing the conversation was going nowhere, and walked away.

"Did you lose anything while you were gone?" He asked with a knowing smirk on his face. I stopped in my tracks.

"Anything like what?" I asked, playing coy.

"Like your ring that I spent good money on." He held up the ring. "How could you be so careless, Harper? It was delivered here while you were out galivanting the streets with your Bride Tribe."

His mentioning the group chat on my phone made me more curious about it than his ring showing up here.

"I was going to tell you that I lost it, but I wanted to recheck my luggage just to be sure." I lied

"Why was it not on your finger? I placed it there as a permanent reminder for the world." I cocked my eyebrow at him.

"And here I was thinking you placed it there as a symbol of your love for me." His eyes widened.

"Don't do that, Harper. Don't try to flip this on me. You are the one who was doing bald-headed slut shit with your friends." His proper tone made the words sound filthier than carpet on a sucker.

"And yet there have been no pictures or videos of

me being a slut or bald-headed, anywhere!" I tossed back as I walked into the kitchen.

The silence that followed felt good. He ordered takeout from his favorite place, plated the food, and set the table. Once we sat, he started talking, but when the first thing out of his mouth wasn't an apology, I tuned him out. He talked about work, meetings, and a promotion that required a photo for the company's "power couples" campaign. I nodded in all the right places, but my head was back in Vegas, where laughter came easily and choices weren't filtered through Karter's opinion.

When he finally stood to clear the table, my phone buzzed. I turned it face down, but not fast enough.

Karter raised a brow. "Who's texting you this late?"

"No one."

"Let me see."

My spine went stiff. "Excuse me?" He had never checked my phone. Or at least that I knew of. But how did he know the name of the group chat?

He held out his hand as if I were a child with something sharp. "Let me see the phone, Harper. You're acting strange, and I'd rather not guess why."

"You don't need to see my phone."

"Then tell me what you're hiding."

"Privacy," I said, standing up. "That's what I'm hiding."

He exhaled through his nose, slow, deliberate, like he was counting. "You always do this. I allow you to go out with your little friends, and you come back acting like you're some independent heathen."

"Excuse you? Did you say you allow me to do something?" I knew he was baiting me for a fight, but I wasn't going to give him the satisfaction, especially when I was dancing on tabletops less than twelve hours ago.

"You're right. I always do this," I echoed. "So, let's not!"

He smiled again, the kind that apologized without meaning it. "I'm not trying to control you."

"You're doing a terrible job convincing me otherwise."

"Harper." He stepped closer. "I love you. I need to know you're not making reckless choices that could ruin us."

The word *us* landed like a leash.

"You mean ruin your image, don't you?" My tone is even and commanding.

"Exactly." He said before he could catch it. "Wait. No Harper. You know that's not what I meant." He tried to grab my waist.

I slipped past him, heading toward the bedroom. "I'm tired. We can talk tomorrow."

Behind me, his voice dropped to that too-calm tone that always made my skin crawl. "The wedding's in three weeks, Harper. Maybe you should focus on that instead of whatever this mood is."

I stopped at the doorway, forcing a smile over my shoulder. "You're right. I'll focus."

He smiled, satisfied, and disappeared into his office.

The second he was gone, I checked the phone.

Xion: 18 Days. Mrs. Pierce. Did you make it home safely?

I stared at it until my eyes blurred. My heart shouldn't have sped up. My lips shouldn't have curved into a smile, but there it was, the quiet thrill of someone asking because they cared, not because they needed to control me.

My thumbs hovered before I finally typed:

Me: I'm home.

Then three dots appeared.

Xion: Glad to hear it, Mrs. Pierce.
Don't unpack too much.

I laughed under my breath, small, scared, and free all at once.

"What's funny?" Karter's voice floated out from the office.

"Nothing," I called back,

But inside, all of me was starting to enjoy the sound of this countdown.

CHAPTER FIVE

Control Issues

Today, the argument started over the color of napkins. Something so small it didn't deserve the tension it caused, but with Karter, every "no" was a symbol of defiance to him.

"I just think ivory looks better with the venue lighting," I said, scrolling through options on my laptop. "The white is too bright for the other colors to blend with."

"Harper." His voice cut through mine, calm but final. "We already agreed on white."

"We? Who's we? I disagreed with white." I said. "And you picked it, tried to pick it anyway.

He didn't look up from his tablet. "Same thing."

That sentence hit like a slap dressed as logic.

"Karter, this is my wedding too! Or did you forget there needs to be a bride to walk down the aisle?"

He sighed like I was exhausting him. "You know I don't care about color schemes. I just need everything to look clean and professional. That's your brand."

"My *brand*?"

He smiled the way people do when they think you're being sensitive. "Baby, that's a compliment. You're polished, pure, refined, and people notice that. You don't need chaos."

"Are you kidding me right now, Karter. I'm a person, not a niche, not a build a bride, not a brand. A damn person." I stared at him, wishing his head would explode.

He finally looked up, brow furrowing. "Why are you getting so emotional about napkins?"

"Because it's not about napkins!" My voice rose. "You don't want me to plan my own wedding. You want to approve it."

He set his tablet down carefully. "That's not true."

"It is." I stood, crossing my arms. "Every decision turns into a presentation. The flowers, the playlist, the vows—you even rewrote half of mine because you said they were 'too personal.' Who does that?"

"I was trying to help you sound more confident," he said smoothly. "You were overthinking them."

"No, I just *think*. You should try it sometime,

without a spreadsheet." I laughed short, sharp, dangerous.

That earned me silence. His jaw tightened, his eyes cooled. I could see the anger begin to bubble up.

Finally, he said, "If you don't like how I do things, maybe you shouldn't have agreed to marry me."

And there it was. The invisible leash he never stopped pulling.

I grabbed my bag and keys. "Maybe I shouldn't have."

"Where are you going?"

"To clear my head."

"Don't stay gone long."

"I wasn't planning to."

He didn't stop me, just watched me leave like a man confident the door would swing back open on its own. I sat in the car, gripping the wheel until the shaking in my hands subsided. The sparkle of his plain ring caught the light, and I missed the way Xion's ring sparkled. And like he knew I was thinking about him, my phone vibrated.

> Xion: You look better when you're smiling.

I looked around to see if I could see him. How did he always know when something was wrong?

You stalking me now?

Xion: Nah. Just watching you realize that you've outgrown your current situation.

You think you know everything.

Xion: I don't. But I know freedom when I see it trying to breathe.

Mama's house soothed me the moment I walked in, warm, loud, cluttered in all the comforting ways only home could be.

"Look at you, Miss Fancy," she teased, tugging me into a hug that smelled like cocoa butter and greens. "You look like stress, wrapped in Chanel."

"Probably accurate."

"You hungry?" She said, turning back into the kitchen.

"I could eat." I shrugged.

"Good. I made too much, as usual." She smiled.

As we sat down, she handed me a plate that could cure child hunger.

"So," she said casually, "you still marrying that man?"

"Mama."

"Don't 'Mama' me. You look miserable. You talk about that man like you're his employee."

"He's just... particular."

"That's the polite way to say controlling." She snorted.

"He means well." I picked at the chicken on my plate

"Meaning well and doing well ain't the same thing, Harper." She leaned forward. "You ain't gotta be with somebody who organizes your joy." That one stung.

"You think I don't know that?" I snipped.

"Knowing and leaving ain't the same thing, baby," she said gently. Mama always knew when to push and when to retreat to keep up roped into serious conversations.

"He makes me feel like everything I do is wrong. Like I'm too emotional, too impulsive. Like if I'd just follow the plan, things would be perfect." I sighed, blinking fast.

"And whose plan is it?"

"His," I admitted to myself more than to her.

"You always wanted love to look like it did in the '90s movies. But they don't make love like that anymore. Nowadays, love finds you in the most unexpected ways. " Mama's voice softened.

I sat there, quiet, letting her words sit heavy in the air.

After finishing dinner with Mama, I decided to have a conversation with Lessa. I hadn't spoken to her since we got back from Vegas, but I hadn't forgotten about the way she was looking while we were there.

"Hey stranger," she answered, music thumping faintly in the background.

"Hey, boo," I said. "What are you up to? You have a minute to talk?"

"Girl nothing, and for you? Always. You sound... off. Karter trippin' again?"

"When is he not?" I muttered.

She laughed low. "Valid. Girl, you sound *tired.*"

"I am." I hesitated. "Leesa, what was going on with Harley in Vegas?"

The music in the background stopped. "Uh... what you mean?"

"I peeped the way you looked at her at the table like

you knew something I didn't. Then she was acting weird, distant even. Like she was hiding something. And when I tried to talk about it last night, she brushed me off."

Leesa went quiet for a beat too long.

"Leesa."

"Harper, don't make me the middleman." She sighed.

"So there *is* something." I was trying to maintain my composure but I was getting more anxious by the minute.

"Girl, I'm not saying that."

"So what are you saying? Because you're not denying it either."

"Look..." Her voice softened. "You know I love Harley, but she's been off lately. That whole weekend felt... staged. Like everybody was performing happy. Even her."

"Performing for who?" My chest tightened.

"Maybe for you," she said quietly. "Maybe for Karter."

"Why would she need to perform for him?" I blinked, gripping the phone harder.

"Ask yourself that," she murmured. "But be ready for the answer."

The line went silent except for my own breath.

"Leesa, you have never been one to lie to me. So please, tell me whatever you know.

"Look, I don't know if there is something but I know there has been a lot of back and forth between Karter and Harley lately." My heart dropped.

Was there something going on with Karter and Harley that I couldn't see. Was I too close to see what is going on around me?

On the drive back, I replayed everything—Harley's smiles that didn't reach her eyes, the secretive glances between her and Karter at the engagement dinner, the sudden topic changes when I walked into the room.

The glances, fragments of conversations, lingering stares, all things I hadn't wanted to see because pretending was easier. But now, knowing was going to lead me to freedom.

When I got home, Karter was waiting, leaning against the counter with that calm that felt like bait.

"Where were you?" His voice was annoying.

"Out!" I snapped.

"You were supposed to be home by six.".

"It's barely seven." I rolled my eyes

"You know I don't like surprises." He smiled wickedly.

"Well," I said, brushing past him, "maybe you shouldn't be marrying me."

"You always twist my words, Harper." He caught my wrist gently, but firm enough to make my pulse jump as I walked past him.

"Maybe because they're always double-sided." I turned and stared him down.

"You're tired. Maybe you should go take a bath. Harley came by to drop off some items for you to restock your bath essentials while you were gone." He dropped my wrist slowly, smiling again.

Karter mentioning Harley being in the house after I was gone made my breath hitch. I walked away without another word, locking the bathroom door behind me.

When I finally sat on the edge of the tub, my phone buzzed and my heart surged a little.

Xion: 15 Days, Mrs. Pierce. Are you still pretending?

I stared at my reflection, at the woman who looked exhausted and alive for the first time in months.

Not for long.

Xion: That's my girl.

CHAPTER SIX

Pieces of the Night

Pieces of the Night

The next morning started quietly. Karter had already left for work, his side of the bed crisp like he hadn't slept there at all. I stretched, happy to be alone for once, then I rolled over and climbed out of the bed and did a little happy dance. A lot was swirling in my head about the way Karter, Harley, and I needed to sit down and call her at some point today.

Deciding to take a warm bath while I was alone granted me the time to clear my head before I got into anything with my sister. I ran the water and let the heat ground me in my thoughts while I unpacked the clown-sized bag of fuckery.

When my mind was clear, I went to make myself some breakfast for the first time since we moved into this giant condo seven months ago. Walking in the kitchen, my stomach dropped. There was a note sitting on the counter beside my coffee mug.

Breakfast is in the warmer. Don't forget the cake tasting at two o'clock. Try not to embarrass me by being on CP time. — K.

I rolled my eyes so hard it hurt. He was starting to sound like an old woman with all his nagging and rules. Embarrass him, like him still wearing penny loafers wasn't an embarrassment in itself?

He always did this. Try to gaslight me into thinking that I am embarrassing him when what he was really saying was, "Stop noticing that I'm controlling you."

The air in the condo felt heavy, so I decided to make it lighter by starting a fight I knew was overdue.

I video called Harley and prepared to dump the bag of fuckery in front of her, force her to admit what she's been doing, then cut her off. She answered on the third ring, fresh-faced and glowing. I had to admit, deceit looked good on her.

"Well, good morning, soon-to-be Mrs. Peoples!" she chirped.

"Hey. You busy?" I smiled tightly.

"Not really. What's up?"

"I wanted to ask you something about Vegas."

Her eyes flickered, just for a second. "Oh boy, here we go. What about it?"

"You were acting... weird. You and Karter both. And now that I'm back, I can't shake the feeling that everyone knows something I don't."

"Girl, you're just anxious. You always get like this before big life stuff." She laughed, fake with a nervous undertone.

"That's not what this is," I said softly. "Be honest with me, Harley. Did something happen?"

Her tone changed, still sweet, but with an edge. "Harper, you've always been dramatic. You overthink, twist people's words, and then you end up hurting yourself. Karter told me you've been really stressed. Maybe talk to him instead of making up stories in that little head of yours."

"So now you and Karter talk about *me?*" The mere idea of Karter made my stomach twist.

"You're my sister, silly," she said quickly. "We both just want what's best for you."

"We? So now you and Karter are a fucking team. And you're defending him? What the hell, Harley?"

"I'm defending your relationship. You know how hard it was for him to get where he is. You can't keep second-guessing him every time he tries to help you."

"Help me?" I snapped. "He doesn't want to help! Is that what you think? Well, let me tell you, he isn't trying to help me; he wants to control me. He rewrote my vows, Harley. He told me what to wear to my own bridal shower!"

"You're being ungrateful. He's trying to make things perfect for you." She sighed, exasperated.

"Perfect for who?"

"For *you*, Harper!" she said louder. "He knows how to keep things organized. He's structured. And you need to admit that you've always needed that kind of balance. You're too emotional sometimes."

I stared at her, realizing she wasn't hearing me because she was too busy repeating him.

"You sound just like him," I whispered.

"Then maybe, just maybe, it's because he's right." She smiled faintly.

The line went silent. My throat burned.

"You know what you're right." I said quietly, "I'll keep my mouth shut and be a good little puppet with his hand up my ass!"

"Harper. Quit being dramatic. Nobody is trying to control you. We are simply trying to help."

"Sure, you are!" I scoffed. The longer I stayed on this phone, the more I wanted to hang up in her face.

Harley's expression faltered for a blink, then smoothed back into a practiced sisterly calm. "You're tired. Get some rest before the tasting. Love you."

She hung up before I could say it back.

That bitch. If I didn't think something was already going on, this would have confirmed it.

Walking into the cake tasting, I made sure that I was through the door right at two o'clock. Karter had his face in his phone as usual, so I snuck up behind him only to see a text from Harley come through on his phone.

Harley: We need to talk. I think Harper knows!

Instead of acknowledging the message, I stepped back and cleared my throat. He jumped, closing the phone quickly, trying to hide what I've already seen.

"Look at you. Making it just in time to start the tasting." He said, standing and pulling out my seat.

"I was here before two, but you were so engrossed with your phone, I didn't want to interrupt you," I said sweetly.

He inhaled a bit, and I knew that I had all the answers that I needed. I just needed to get through this cake tasting. Ten flavors later, Karter had decided on the flavor for the groom's cake. Normally, he would disagree with everything I liked, but today, for some reason, he was tame and gave actual feedback on the different cake flavors. When he decided to go with Red Velvet, I asked him if he was sure, reminding him how he turned it down when I originally picked it for him.

"Harper, I should have trusted you when you chose it. That was one of your better suggestions for sure." Karter sure knew how to give the most backhanded compliments.

To save face, I smiled and prepared to leave because tonight he was going to be in the hot seat!

When Karter came home that evening, I was waiting for him in the living room, arms crossed. I had packed a few of my belongings when I got back to the house and put them in the trunk of my car. Xion's words echoed in my head as I walked back into the house.

Don't unpack too much.

Now I sat there waiting and knew it was time for action when I heard the key turn the lock.

"We need to talk," I said before his second foot crossed the threshold.

"About what?" He kissed my forehead like I'd said hello.

"Harley."

He paused, smile flickering. "What about her?"

"She said you two talk about me. About my stress, my emotions, things going on with me that aren't her business." I said, hoping he would take the bait.

"Harper, you sound paranoid." He chuckled lightly, like I was adorable.

"Paranoid?" My laugh sounded sinister. "Don't call me that!"

"Calm down, okay. I only talk to your sister because she worries about you. Everyone does. Summer and Leesa do too. We can see what you can't. You've been off lately, distant, and moody. Some would even say erratic." He raised both hands, like he was trying to calm me.

"Erratic?" I echoed, voice shaking. "What makes me erratic? Huh? Not letting you plan every breath I take? Or is it me wanting to have a say in my own life?"

He tilted his head. "Everything I do is what keeps us from falling apart."

"You can thank me later." He said, walking away.

There it was, the line that made my skin crawl every time: the way he said *us* when he meant *me*.

"You make everything sound like it's my fault." I turned away, fighting tears.

He stepped closer, lowering his voice. "No, baby. I know what happens when you start overthinking. You spiral. And I can't watch you ruin the best thing that's ever happened to you."

"Now breathe, Harper? You're safe." His hand brushed my arm, gentle but heavy.

I froze, feeling anything but safe.

After he went to shower, I sat at my desk to clear my head and saw a new email notification. My eyes grew to the size of saucers when I saw the subject line. My heart stopped, my palms began to sweat and the room was all of a sudden too hot. It was an email from Karter's company for Karter's boss. Had he told them about me? Did he know that they were making this request?

Opportunity: Private Wedding Coordination for CEO of P&P Corporation

From: events@P&PCorp.org

Ms. Moore,

Our CEO and his fiancé are seeking a private event planner for their upcoming wedding. You came highly recommended and your portfolio impressed the team. We'd love to discuss a contract if you're available this week.

Please let me know as soon as possible as this is a time sensitive matter.

Best,

Felicia Harris
Executive Assistant, P&P Corp.

For a moment, pride broke through the fog. This was huge. If I landed that wedding, everything would change. My name, my business, my independence. The last part sat heavily on my spirit. Was that what Karter was afraid of? My independence leading to my freedom? But then another thought hit me. What is Karter going to say about this? And why hadn't he *told* me?

That night, after Karter fell asleep, I sat in the dark with my phone glowing in my hand. My thumbs hovered before I texted *him*.

Are you sleeping?

Xion: Not yet. Was just about to text you. But it was nice to see I was on your mind tonight.

I smiled before responding.

I got an email today. It was a job offer.

Xion: You sound hesitant.

It's to plan a wedding for the CEO of P&P Corp., Karter's company.

Xion: That's big. Congratulations.

Thanks. I think Karter may be upset when he finds out.

Xion: Why would he be upset? He should be happy that he may potentially rub elbows with a CEO.

Should be, but not everyone knows how to clap for others. It's an excellent opportunity for me, and I can't wait to meet with them.

Xion: It's your opportunity. Not his. Please, don't make it about him.

You make everything sound so simple.

Xion: It is simple. You keep pretending it's complicated because you've been conditioned to shrink so that others can shine.

I don't know how to tell him I got it.

Xion: Then don't tell him. You don't owe him your good news. You tell the first person that comes to mind when you feel happy. But looks like you already did.

My fingers hovered over the keyboard, trembling.

> Cocky much. 😅 I shouldn't be telling you this.

Xion: Not cocky, proud of my wife. And you already told me now. No take-backs. That means you're already choosing yourself.

THE PHONE BUZZED AGAIN.

Xion: 14 Days, Mrs. Pierce. I'm proud of you!

I leaned back on the couch, heart racing and soft all at once.

For the first time, I realized something terrifying and beautiful.

I wasn't afraid of time running out.

I was afraid of what might happen if I actually let it.

CHAPTER SEVEN

Cracks in the Frame

Three days later, I sat in the office space that had been dedicated to me in Karter's building. I had signed the contract to plan the wedding for the CEO the day after I got the email, and was told to start immediately. He and his fiancé were busy with other tasks, but I was given complete creative control over the wedding. The instructions from Felicia were for me to plan this wedding based on my vision for a fairytale wedding.

I wondered what kind of woman didn't want to be involved with her own wedding, but Felica assured me the wedding was more of a surprise for the bride. The magnitude of the project felt like a lot, but I was up for the challenge. I had eleven days to plan the wedding of the century. I pulled out all the stops to make sure that this wedding was going to go off without a hitch. I had thrown planning my own wedding to the side to make sure this one was perfect.

Karter found out about me planning the wedding by accident. He came in one night, and I had wedding dress ideas for the bride already picked out. I was in the process of sending them over to Felicia when he walked in. When I told him about the opportunity, instead of congratulating me, he sat me down and gave me a stern talking to. Making sure I understood the importance of doing a good job because it will reflect poorly on him if I don't.

After our talk, I threw myself into my work. I'd stopped sleeping next to Karter. I told him I needed space to create, but really, I needed room to breathe. He'd started noticing the little things first. The way I didn't flinch when he raised his voice. Didn't hurry to answer his texts, and my yeses had turned into *we'll sees*. It felt good to be in control of my life, without him lingering over me for a change.

Karter didn't know it yet but his most prized possession was slowly slipping out of his grasp.

Karter showed up at my job unannounced, flowers in hand, smile wide enough to fool those who didn't know him.

"Thought I'd surprise my fiancé," he said loud enough for everyone to hear.

I hadn't been in the office a week yet and he was already trying lay claim to me like everyone didn't know we were together.

"At ten in the morning?" I blinked embarrassed see him.

"Wanted to check on you." He said before stepping in my temporary office and closing the door.

"I noticed you left early yesterday." He said as soon as the doors latch caught.

"You mean I got off at five?" I forced a polite laugh.

"We leave when everyone else leaves here, we stay until the days tasks are done." He leaned in, lowering his voice.

"Well, I should have left at noon then. I only stayed to five to help Amy with a proposal presentation she needed to finish." I still smiling. I could tell my pleasantries were killing him. "We will talk about this later at lunch?" His jaw flexed, but that plastered smile never broke.

"I'm busy later." I could tell that he was ready to explode.

"Busy, with what?"

"With work. Or would you like like to tell the CEO that I couldn't send him the venue to finalize because you wanted to take me to lunch to scold me?" I could see the gears turning behind his mechanical mind.

He chuckled, low and dangerous. "Cute." Then, through gritted teeth, "Let's not forget the reason that you got this job."

"I got this job because of my portfolio. They didn't even know you and I knew each other until I asked if it would be a conflict of interest." I made sure to look in his eyes and watch his ego deflate.

He froze for half a second, opened the door and then kissed my cheek for the audience watching. "See you at home, baby."

When he left, my coworkers pretended not to stare. But everyone saw it, the crack beneath the picture-perfect engagement.

That night, I came home to candles lit, wine poured, and music playing softly. For a second, it almost felt normal. Until he said: "Why's your sister calling me so much?"

"Excuse me?" I stopped mid-step.

"Harley," he said, swirling his glass. "She called me twice today. Wanted to 'check in.' Funny, right?"

"Nobody is laughing so I guess not! Is there anything else?" I asked annoyed.

He smiled. "She said you've been distant. And the thinks you may be having cold feet."

"Is there a question in there somewhere?"

"Are you? Having cold feet that is. Because if so, we need to fix that!"

"You tell me." I stared at him, voice cold.

He took a sip, eyes narrowing. "Don't make me regret loving you, Harper."

"You mean you don't already? Sheesh. I've been reading the room wrong."

He slammed the glass down, red wine bleeding across the marble like it was wounded.

"God, you're so dramatic."

I turned toward the stairs, fighting the tremor in my hands. "That doesn't work, not anymore. If anyone is dramatic it's Harley. So worried about me that she called you instead of me. Birds of a feather!" I tossed the last bit over my shoulder as I walked with my head high up the stairs.

Upstairs, I went into the guest room I had been staying in, locked the door behind me and grabbed my phone out my pocket. Karter was an absolute asshole. Who sets the mood to ambush and argue with somebody? A lunatic that's who. I was so pissed off that I wanted to call and curse Harley out. But I stopped when I realized there was one message waited.

Xion: How are you doing Mrs. Pierce?

I'm alright X.

Xion: Is that my new nickname?

Maybe, do you like it? How was your day?

Xion: Um.. Is this Harper?

Yesss..

Xion: I need visual proof.

Just then a facetime call came through from Xion. I

grabbed my headphones and put one in my ear. Checking my hair before I answer.

When the call connected all I could see was a singular eyeball.

He pulled the phone back allowing me to see his whole face as I tried to stop laughing at him. He was even more handsome than I remembered in a grey button down shirt and his gold chain glinting against his beautiful skin.

I stared at the screen for a minute until I remembered to breathe.

"Damn you're beautiful." He said. I didn't want to risk Karter eaves dropping, so I texted my response to him. I could see him read the message at the top of his screen and his brows furrowed. I could see the moment it clicked, that I was texting to keep from speaking. He nodded and answered me.

Don't flatter me like that Mr. Pierce.

"Ahhh, so today I'm Mr. Pierce. Okay Mrs. Pierce." My cheeks heated at his words.

You didn't answer my question.

"What question Harper?"

How was your day?

"It was okay. I have a huge project I'm working on but I am totally hands off for a change. I have an intern doing all the work so I am forced to sit back and see what she comes up with.

> Must be hard for you to not be the one in charge of things.

"Nah I am used to allowing people to function in their lane. We all have a job to do and I allow everyone to do their share. I only interfere when necessary.

> That's respectable.

"Now tell me how your day was and how the new job is going."

I could see my eyes light up when it was my turn to talk about my day. Fearing it would be too much to type I decided to speak instead. Luckily I heard the door close at the same time Xion was asking how the new job was going.

"My day was pretty chill. I have gotten so much done over the last few days that I am actually ahead of the game. At first I was a little worried about them giving me creative control to curate the wedding of their dreams, but after a few approvals I am more confident now." I beam while speaking about my dream job.

"Look who has a beautiful voice to match her beautiful face." He laughed. "The last time we spoke you sounded like DMX a little." I burst out laughing at him.

"I love that smile." He said looking at me like he could eat me.

"Thank you."

"So where did you get the inspiration for this wedding you're planning?" He asked.

"Truthfully?" I looked at him deciding if I wanted to share with him or not.

"Honesty is key."

"I'm basically planning my dream wedding. From the location to the colors. It was all the wedding I had planned for myself for years. But when I told Karter about all the ideas he basically told me to start over. When I got this oppurtunity I decided that if I wasn't going to get to walk down the aisle in the Vera Wang dress on my Pinterest board, that somebody should." I admitted.

He sat there for a minute and I wasn't sure if he was judging me or feeling sorry for me.

"Damn. That's heavy, Harper. But selfless as well. To plan your dream for somebody else has to be hard." I could feel the concern in his voice.

"At first I was sad letting go of my memories but when I really got into it I was excited. I was doing what I was born to do and planning things the way that I envisioned them. So i'm good now. Its kind of my therapy right now. Just sucks I won't get to see it because my wedding is the same day." I laughed.

I heard the door down stairs and knew Karter had come back, so I knew it was time to hang up the phone.

"I have to go now." I reluctantly said, before he could start another conversation.

"Well I will talk to you soon. Mrs. Pierce oh and if I haven't said it today. 11 Days!" He smiled again before ending the call.

I sat there flustered. The heat of his gaze had my entire body tingling. I hadn't felt that way in years, and now that I remembered, it was going to be hard to not crave the feeling again. I set the phone down, heart pounding so loud I could hear it in my ears.

From the hallway, Karter's voice floated up. "Harper, you hungry?"

"No!" I swallowed.

"Don't be a child, Harper. You need to eat!" he called, footsteps fading.

I walked over to the window to close the blinds when I noticed it.

Across the street, a black SUV idled under the streetlight. The tinted windows shielded the person inside, and the engine was quiet.

My phone buzzed again.

Xion: He's there for your protection.
Don't be afraid.

I gasped, looking out again, but the SUV was gone.

CHAPTER EIGHT

I Love You Not

The next morning, I woke up feeling horrible. My head throbbed, my throat felt like I had swallowed a brillo pad, and, combined with the mental fatigue of my current situation with Karter, my body was screaming for a break.

I called Felicia, hoping my voice didn't sound too bad. When she answered, I tried my best to explain to her what was going on. But she stopped me mid-sentence.

"Harper, is that you? Oh, honey, you sound horrible. Please take the time needed to feel better. You've already finalized all the plans. All that's left to do is to make sure the bride gets everything that she needs. Hell, you've earned a day off, Harper." I thanked her as best I could before ending the call.

I lay on the couch wrapped in a blanket, watching

the ceiling fan spin in a slow circle above me. Every time I closed my eyes, I saw Xion's face on that screen. His laugh, his steady eyes, that voice saying *eleven days*. My stomach growled, reminding me that I needed to eat, when the doorbell rang. I took my time sitting up because nobody should be coming over, since lately Karter and I had been working.

When the knock followed the doorbell, I decided to open it. I padded over to the door to find a very handsome, tall, dark-skinned man standing there, holding a bag of food.

"This is for you, Mrs. Pierce. Mr. Pierce wanted to make sure that you ate." I smiled before taking the bag. But I couldn't help but wonder how he always knew what I needed.

I reached for my phone, and thought about texting him, then stopped when I saw the bubbles in the messages already.

> Xion: Good Morning, Beautiful. I see
> you didn't go to work today, so I
> decided to send you breakfast.

I smiled at the gesture before reaching out and taking the food from the man.

"Thank you, Sir." I flashed a smile at him.

"Name's Leo, ma'am.. And you're welcome." He turned away, leaving as quickly as he had come.

I went back into the house and was about to dive into my food, but not before thanking Xion.

> Thank you again for the food. I don't feel well today, so this soup is about to hit the spot.

I didn't know why I felt the need to tell him about being sick, but it was just so easy to talk to him. When I heard a chime, I looked at my phone, but quickly realized it wasn't my phone that had the notification. When the reminder sound chimed again, it was the chime of Karter's iPad from the kitchen counter.

Three soft pings, one after another.

Typically, I would have ignored it, but after the way that Karter had been acting lately, something was pulling me to look at it. So I did. I half-expected to see the iPad locked, but when I picked it up, the screen was already open to the message thread. I did a double-take when I saw her name. This Hoey hoe box!

> Harley 💋

I let out a nervous laugh and couldn't figure out why it felt like my body was on fire. I scrolled up on the messages because now that I knew, I had to learn the whole story.

At first, I only saw one line of the latest message:

> Karter: I miss you. Last night shouldn't have ended.

The breath left my body. My thumb hovered, trembling, then scrolled up.

> Karter: You're driving me crazy, Harley. You know I can't focus when you wear that robe.

> Harley 💋: Stop pretending you don't like it. You came over knowing what you wanted.

> Karter: Harper's still asleep. We have time.

I felt my stomach twist before I began to dry heave for air. There was nothing in my stomach to come up, but my body wouldn't stop until it spewed stomach acid. After cleaning myself up, I picked up the iPad and I scrolled faster, eyes blurring as message after message confirmed what my heart had been whispering for weeks.

There were photos of them together and some alone. The videos were sickening to watch. Seeing him jack his uncircumcised dick made me want to rip my eyes out. Then there were the midnight texts, going back for months.

The whole time I was planning my wedding, my sister was sleeping with my fiancé.

I dropped the iPad like it burned me. My hands shook so hard I pressed them against my mouth to stop the sound that was clawing its way out of me. Did I confront my back-stabbing slut of a sister first or Captain Hoodie's lying, dawg ass?

I picked up my phone to give Karter a piece of my mind, but when I did, my mother's face was bouncing around the screen. I answered the phone and immediately pressed the video call option. When the call connected, I could see her sitting in a hospital bed, and my world stopped.

"Mama, is everything okay?" She rolled her eyes, as if my concern was bothering her.

"I am fine, Harper. I was in the grocery store with Delores and had a little spell. I just wanted to call you before you heard it from somebody else." I sighed, happy she was okay, but I was still going to where she was.

"What hospital, Mama?" That was all I could say before Ms. Delores, my mother's best friend and nosey neighbor, took the phone from Mama's hands.

"Hey, Harper baby. Your mama is under explaining as usual. She didn't just have a spell. She was talking to me one minute, and then the next she was on the ground having a seizure." My brain went blank. It had been years since my mother had a seizure, but I knew if she was having them, that something was wrong.

Remembering that we share locations, I pulled up hers since neither of them had told me theirs. As they continued bickering, I sent a text to Xion, hoping whoever he had in the SUV was nearby to take me to my mother.

> Hey, the man in the car. Can he take me to the hospital?"

His response was instant.

> Xion: He is pulling up now. Is everything okay? Do I need to come to you?"

I could feel his concern, and I wanted to ease his mind.

> I'm fine. I need to get to my mother, but I still don't feel well enough to drive to her.

Xion: He's at the door. Go ahead, and
he will help you to the car.

Thank you, X.

Xion: Anything for my wife.

I disconnected the call as they started talking about something else, forgetting me completely. I found myself blushing as I walked out the door, grabbing my purse and the iPad on the way out.

L eo helped me in the car, and we headed out. I connected to the car's Bluetooth and used the GPS to get me to my mother. By the time she sent her location, I was five minutes out. I would usually call Harley to let her know what was going on, but I needed a moment to speak to my mother about what I had found on the iPad. Remembering that Karter could see the location, I quickly put it on airplane mode.

As we pulled up to the emergency room, I could see Ms. Delores walking out the front doors. I hopped out of the car as soon as Leo stopped. I darted across the walkway, moving as fast as I could, to get to Ms. Delores.

"Hey, Ms. Delores. Can you tell me where my mother is?" She looked shocked to see me.

"Oh, hey, baby. Are you okay? You look a little under the weather yourself." She says, pulling me into a hug.

"I am fine, I just want to know where my mother is," I said, stepping back out of the hug.

Leo appeared behind me, holding my purse and the iPad. I had been moving so fast that I didn't realize that I hadn't grabbed my things out of the car.

"Do you know this tall cup of decaf?" Ms. Delores practically purred.

"Yes, this is Leo." He smiled and winked at Ms. Delores.

The way that she looked at him was like she could devour him and his soul whole.

"My mother?" I said, breaking her out of whatever trance she had slipped into.

"Oh, they are admitting her. I was coming out here to call you and your sister and let you guys know that they are going to keep her overnight." I looked at her.

"Did you already call Harley?" I asked her, hoping that she hadn't.

"Well, I didn't get a chance to because you came running up to me as soon as I got out the door." I laughed a little, relieved, I wouldn't have to see my sister right now.

"Tell me what room she is going to be in, and I will let Harley know." I lied.

"She is going to be in room 534." The room number made me flash back to Vegas.

"Okay, baby. Since you are here, I am going to the house to get myself together. It has been a long day, and I need a drink. Your mama scared the hell out of me today." She said letting her true feelings out.

"Thank you, Ms. Delores. You have always been such a big help with her. I will send you a little something. Don't worry about feeding them grand babies tonight. Dinner will be on me." Her eyes lit up.

"You don't have to tell me twice. I need a night off anyway." She said, hugging me again.

"I will keep you updated on her status when I get up there." Ms Delores smiled, before walking away.

I turned to Leo as she walked in the direction of her car.

"Thank you so much for bringing me. Can I tip you?" I asked.

"Mrs. Pierce, I am paid handsomely. Anything you need I am here to provide." I tilted my head to the side because surely he didn't mean anything.

When I got to my mother's room, I could hear her telling the nurses how they do their jobs.

"Little girl, you already stuck me 2 times, and you missed the vein both times. Now go find me somebody else because clearly you think I'm a damn pincushion." I shook my head as I walked into the room.

"Nurses make the worst patients," I say, looking at her, announcing my presence.

"No, we don't. We can just identify when somebody is incompetent." I rolled my eyes before addressing the nurse.

"Hi, I'm Harper, her daughter. Please forgive her." I said, extending my hand to the tech. Instead of shaking it, she scoffed and walked off like I was the one who insulted her.

"See, I told you. In-comp-e-tent!" My mother stretched the word out as the nurse left the room.

"Mama. Cut it out. These people are not going to want to help you if you keep this mess up." I remind her.

"And who gives a damn. I have worked in this hospital longer than most of these little heffa's have been wiping their own behinds. I know when they are trying to hurry up and get stuff done so they can get back to looking at the new attending or get back to their phones." I smiled, walked over to her, and kissed her forehead.

"How are you feeling, mama?" I asked, pulling the chair up next to the bed.

"I am fine. I told Delores that, and she insisted on making a big fuss about this." When she looked at me, I could see the fear that she was trying to shove down and maintain her hard exterior.

"Ma you're not fine. Now tell me how long you have been having seizures again. I know if they are back then there is something else going on." I sat next to her waiting for her to tell me what is going on with her.

"There has only been one other incident and I went to the doctor like I am supposed to. So like I said there is nothing to fuss over right now." I nodded, understanding that I wouldn't get more out of her today and would have to wait for the doctor if I wanted to know what was going on.

"Now tell me why you are out of the house looking like this." She said, looking over my clothes.

I had been in such a rush to get to her that I didn't even realize that I was still in my sweats and a crop top. Luckily, I still had my braids in and didn't have to do my hair. My Crocs were multicolored and didn't match anything I had on, but I didn't care. It felt good to go, without having to worry about how I would appear to the world.

"Well, I rushed out of the house to see about you, Mama," I told her.

"Girl, you must think you are talking to one of your little friends. I don't care about those clothes, I am talking about that pain behind the worry in your eyes." Was it that obvious, or was that motherly instinct real, and she could sense the pain I had?

"What do you mean?" I asked, trying to decide if now was the time to tell her about the whore of a daughter she raised.

"Harper. Don't play with me! Now tell me what is going on before I make these alarms go off from whipping your ass in this room!" I blew out a breath and handed her the iPad.

I thought she would have the same reaction as I did. I waited for the disgust to display across her face, but it never came. Instead, she just shook her head.

"So?" I asked.

"So, what are you prepared to do?" She asked me. There was no outrage, no anger, hell, almost no shock.

"What do you mean? I am ready to kill your daughter for being a whore and leave this asshole where he stands." I barked.

"First, mind your tongue. I know you're upset, but let's not forget that I will still break both of my feet off in your ass. Second, why did it take this long for you to want to leave him? You have been miserable for months, and you drew the line in the sand at him sleeping with your sister? " Was she fucking serious right now. This dog was literally carrying on with my sister behind my back for months and acted like it was nothing.

"Seriously, Mama?"

"Harper. You let this man disrespect you at every turn. The way he speaks down to you, the way that he controls your life, hell, even the way that you eat. But when he disrespects you by sleeping with your sister, you want to be overly upset. I told you when you were growing up that if you let someone run over you one time, you give them the power to keep running over you. How was he supposed to know where the line was when you let him trample all over you?" I was about to speak, but she looked at me, prompting me to shut my mouth.

"Now I have let you live your life and not interfered, but now I see that was the wrong thing to do. Your sister and Karter are pieces of shit for what they did, but I need to know what you are going to do now that the rose-colored glasses have been removed. You have ten days to decide, Harper." She sat up waiting for a response, and I didn't have one. But hearing her tell me how much time I have spent reminded me of Xion.

"I got married while I was in Vegas." I don't know why this was my response, but the smile that spread across my mother's face was knowing.

etting home that night I was exhausted. Karter wasn't even in the house when I got there, and I was relieved to be able to unpack the day without any interruptions or the third degree about where I had been. My phone pinged twice. I picked it up and had two messages. One from mama and one from Xion. I opened the one from Xion first because I was afraid that my mother had changed her mind about how she felt.

After I told her what happened in Vegas and caught her up with everything I had been dealing with since I got back she was anxious to meet Xion. Calling him her son in Law like she knew this man. I laughed when she went down the rabbit hole about how he should whisk me off my feet at my wedding. But then the room went somber when I realized I needed to figure out how I was going to call off the current wedding happening in ten days.

I opened the message from Xion.

Xion: Just wanted to make sure that you were okay.

Me: Yes, I am. Thanks so much for lending me Leo today. I needed to get to my mom quickly and he came in clutch.

Xion: 😂😂😂 Clutch huh? No worries baby. He is your personal detail so starting today he will take you anywhere you need to go.

Xion: You should see your own black card in you wallet as well. I had him slip it in there when you got out the truck today.

I checked my wallet and sure enough there was a black American Express card in my wallet with the name Haper M. Pierce engraved in it. My eyes grew when I felt the weight of the card in my hands. Like a fortune was just a swipe away.

X what is this? And why does it say Harper Pierce.

Xion: Because that's your name.

Well thank you. For everything.

I switched over to my mother's message and my eyes ballooned again.

Dukes: Girl, there was man that came in here ordering the nurses around and handing out instructions like he was the boss. Said his name was Xane Pierce. Now I am in a private suite and some fancy neurologist will be in to see me in the morning. If this is your Vegas husband then you need to hold on to him!

I sat there for a minute trying to wrap my head around everything. I knew she said Xane but could she have misheard and it be Xion.

Xion, did you move my mother?

I waited for a response from him but it never came.

When Karter came home that evening, I was sitting at the kitchen table, silent, phone face down, iPad neatly placed in front of me.

He smiled when he saw me — that same politician smile.

"Hey, baby. Feeling any better?"

I looked at him. "You left your iPad unlocked."

He froze, keys still in his hand. "What?"

"I said you left it unlocked." My voice didn't shake; it was calm in a way that scared even me.

"Okay..." He took a step forward, frowning. "Did you.."

"Yes." I leaned back. "I saw everything."

The air between us shifted instantly.

"Harper, "

"Don't, Harper, me." I stood, eye to eye with him, every inch of me vibrating with rage. "Don't you dare try to flip this shit on me. I'm not the problem here. You are!"

He opened his mouth, searching for the right lie. "Sugar Lump, it's not what you think."

"I have always hated it when you call me that. And this is exactly what I think!" My voice sliced through the air, sharp enough to slit his throat. "You and Harley? My *sister*? How could you?"

"You've been distant. I was lonely. Harley. She was there." He sighed, trying to steady his voice.

"You don't get to make yourself the victim here, Karter!" My hand slammed the table, making the silverware tremble.

His eyes hardened. "You never gave me the attention I needed, Harper. You've been obsessed with this fake wedding planning career, when it's more like a hobby or a project even. Harley just... understood."

That sentence twisted the knife the two of them stabbed each other with.

"You mean she let you be the god you pretend to be?" I smirked

His jaw flexed. "You're being dramatic again."

"Oh fuck you, Karter!" I shouted. "You cheated on me, and with my sister! You've been lying to my face, using me, controlling me, and now you want to tell me how to *feel*? Well fuck that and fuck you!"

He ran a hand down his face, trying to remain calm. "You're spiraling again. We can talk about this later when you've cooled down."

"Nah," I shrugged. "We're done talking. We're done, period."

I walked past him, and for the first time, he didn't

stop me. Maybe because he saw something in my eyes he couldn't manipulate, something final.

Upstairs, I locked myself in the guest room, fell onto the bed, and shed my first tear since I had learned of the affair. But it wasn't tears of sadness, but tears of release. I was finally about to be free of this man. But one question remained. Was I ready to step into my role as Mrs. Pierce?

At some point, I must have dozed off because when I finally sat up, the room was dark, except for the glow of my phone.

The unread message from Xion beckoned to something in me.

Xion: Yes, I sent my brother to handle things while he was there. I hope that's okay. He said that your mom is doing well. We will have the best neurologist in the country see her in the morning. She's already on a flight and happens to be your sister in law. Don't worry about anything, Mrs. Pierce. Get some rest tonight, we can talk more in the morning.

Tears spilled down my cheeks, but I was smiling through them. Because for the first time, I wasn't mourning what I lost. I was embracing what it feels like to finally be loved.

CHAPTER NINE

New Keys

The next morning, Leo drove me back to the hospital. Mama was already sitting up in bed, bossing the nurses around like she was head of staff instead of the patient. Her I.V. bag barely dripped before she started complaining about how slow it was going.

"Ma, they're doing their best," I said, stepping inside with a bag of breakfast and fresh flowers.

"They'd do better if they stopped moving like snails in quicksand," she muttered, then her face softened when she saw me.

"You look like new money."

"I feel... lighter," I admitted. "Like my body finally caught up with my decision to let go."

"That's not what the chart says," came a new voice from the doorway. I turned and froze.

The woman standing there looked like she stepped out of a Black Excellence magazine.

Honey-brown skin, long micro-locs pulled into a bun, a white coat embroidered with **Dr. Zena Pierce, M.D., Neurology** across the chest, and the kind of calm authority that made you sit up straighter without being told.

"You must be Harper," she said, smiling. "Your husband has told me a lot about you."

The word *husband* hit different on her tongue.

"You're Xion's...?" I stood, shaking her hand.

"Twin brother's wife," she corrected gently. "Xane's my husband. And I'll be your mother's attending for now."

"Well," Mama interrupted, "since y'all done with all the family introductions, can somebody tell me when I'm going home?"

"You're lucky, Mrs. Moore. Your MRI looks clear, and your labs came back stable. I'm going to run one more test today, but if everything holds, you can go home tomorrow morning." Zena laughed softly, pulling the chart closer.

"Tomorrow?" Mama groaned. "Lord, I thought I was getting out today."

"Tonight, you'll rest here," Zena said smoothly,

"and tomorrow, you'll rest at home. But you're under doctor's orders not to stress your daughter out, deal?"

"Depends on how she acts." Mama smirked.

"You see what I deal with?" I shook my head

"The Pierce men attract strong women. I'm learning that runs in the family." Zena smiled knowingly.

Her phone buzzed, and she excused herself, promising to be back in a few hours.

"She's nice," I told Mama.

"She's fine as hell is what she is," Mama said, grinning. "Looks like both of those Pierce men got good taste." I laughed at her antics.

After I left the hospital, I called the one person who had always told me the truth, whether I wanted to hear it or not. Summer. It had been a minute since she and I had spoken. With me planning the wedding for the people I now knew as Xane and Zena, I was swamped. Not to mention, she was always busy at her salon. I knew the conversation was past due, but after talking to Leesa a few weeks ago, I needed to see if she knew anything.

She picked up on the second ring, voice thick with attitude and concern.

"Girl, I've been waiting for your call. You've been ghosting me since we got back."

"I've been... dealing with things."

"What kind of things?"

"The kind that involves my sister and my fiancé being community property."

"I know the fuck you lying."

"Girl, I wish I were."

"Harley?" she said, her voice climbing. "As in your *blood* sister, Harley? Just planned your whole bachelorette in Vegas, Harley? Climbed out the same coochie as you, Harley?"

"On in the same."

"Get the fuck out of here!" she spat with disgust. "How much bail money do you need? Or do you want me to call Tylesha and Twan to meet us at that bitch house? You know, Twan ain't never liked Karter bitch ass, since middle school anyway."

"Girl, don't I know it?"

"Wait, how did you find out?" I was waiting on her to ask. When she did I sent her all the screenshots of their messages that I had sent to myself.

"Oh, they some dirty muthafuckas. And he trust to be cheating with a turtleneck dick? Eww."

"I guess she saved me from having to find out what his dick looked like, until now." I laughed.

"Or, she's the reason that his bum ass wanted to wait until y'all were married to have sex." I sat on that for a minute.

I thought about the time that he told me that we should remain abstinent until after we are married to repent and cleanse our bodies during our relationship. I thought it was sweet at first, but now I'm just glad that I didn't fuck him.

I could almost hear Summer pacing. "I swear to God, Harper, you know the doctor said my blood pressure is borderline high and you trying to make me stroke out."

"I wish I had your energy right now." I laughed.

"Energy? Girl, I got hands. Harley better hope I don't see her before you do, because I'm whoopin' her like she stole the family Bible!"

"You're ridiculous." That laugh came from somewhere deep.

"I'm serious! And that bitch nigga, Karter?

"I told him we're done."

"Good. 'Cause if you change your mind, I know some cousins who don't ask questions."

"Summer!" I laughed again, but my chest warmed. God, I needed her fire.

Then her tone softened. "You didn't deserve that, Harper. Don't let what they did make you forget who you are."

"I'm trying."

"No," she said firmly. "You're *doing*. Big difference."

The next morning, I was back at the office. The team was doing last-minute touch-ups for the CEO's wedding, and I was focused on final details when the elevator doors opened and someone stepped out who made my breath catch. His tall stature towered over the room, and he had broad shoulders. He had the same confident walk that made time slow down.

It took me a moment, but I could have sworn it was Xion. My heart started beating like Jesus had returned, and I was caught in the act of sinning.

But when he got closer, I realized the difference, the sharper jawline, the dimple that only appeared on one side.

"Good morning, Mrs. Pierce," he said, voice smooth as jazz. "I'm Xane, Xion's twin."

"Of course you are." I shook off the feeling, putting a face to the name I had learned from Zena yesterday.

"He wanted to come himself, but he's tied up with business in Atlanta. I'm here to finalize a few details on his behalf." He smiled.

Before I could respond, a familiar voice sliced through the moment.

"Harper!" Karter barked out.

He was in a suit, smiling for the cameras of coworkers who didn't know the whole story. He walked over like we were still together, not realizing that it wasn't his ring on my finger. Last night, after my shower, I pulled the ring out of the drawer and put it back on. The weight felt so right, and I love how elegant it looked with my Ivory sweater and Chocolate slacks I put on today.

"Hey, baby," he said, reaching for my hand. "We need to go over the final seating chart for *our* wedding this weekend."

I didn't miss a beat, aware of the eyes watching, then smiled a smile that wasn't kind.

"Oh, sweetie," I said softly, "we don't have a wedding anymore. You and your whore of a side project canceled that for us, remember! Or did you think I was, what do you call it? Oh yeah, spiraling?" The room went silent.

"Harper, babe, this isn't the place for this." Karter's smile faltered, his jaw ticking.

"No," I said, calmly. "Here is perfect. You told me not to come back to your place this morning, remember? So I won't. In fact, you can keep the condo. Consider it payment for all the fake love I wasted on you."

A few people nearby froze, pretending not to listen.

Karter's face reddened. "You're embarrassing yourself, Harper."

I crossed my arms. "You did that when you climbed into my sister's bed, with that uncircumcised dick and decided to record it."

He opened his mouth, but Xane stepped forward, calm and solid as a wall. "Mrs Pierce, is there a problem here?" he said evenly.

Karter glared. "Excuse me? Who the fuck are you?"

Xane reached into his jacket and handed me a small black envelope containing a gold-embossed keycard and a set of keys.

"These are for your new condo, Harper. You'll find it's fully furnished and everything has been handled."

"Excuse you, asshole? Who the fuck are you? And what condo? Harper, I swear..." Karter blinked.

Xane smiled politely. "Xane Pierce, CEO." He said, looking down at Karter, before continuing. "Is everything good here?" The shock on Karter's face is meme-worthy.

"Oh, I'm sorry, Mr. Pierce. It's a pleasure to meet you." Typical Karter was ready to suck up to the boss.

Instead of Xane acknowledging him, he spoke to me instead.

"My brother doesn't like his wife living somewhere she's unhappy." He winked at me and gestured to the key card.

The word *wife* hit the air like gospel. I saw Karter's face darken, but for once, he had nothing left to say.

"Thank you." I turned to Xane, heart pounding.

"Welcome to the family, Mrs. Pierce." He gave me that same calm Pierce smile before motioning everyone to get back to work.

My phone buzzed, and I knew it was Karter.

Captain Hoodie: You fucking whore. Are you sleeping with my fucking boss's brother? And why the fuck is he saying that you are married?

I laughed before hitting the block button, then sticking the phone back in my purse and getting back to work.

Xane and Zena met me in the lobby when it was time for me to get off, to take me to my new place. I was nervous and excited at the same time. I had been living with Karter for the past 2 years, and I had almost forgotten what it felt like to live alone in peace.

When I walked into the new apartment that night, I stopped dead in the doorway. It was nothing like the sterile condo I shared with Karter. This place was alive, filled with all my personalities. The sunlight spilled through tall windows, landing on walls washed in soft sage green. There were plants everywhere, Monstera curling along shelves, a fiddle leaf Fig standing proud by the window, vases bursting with fresh Lilies.

The air smelled like citrus and cedar-wood. The furniture was warm, bohemian, with woven rugs, matching comfy throws, and splashes of art on every wall. It looked like freedom had hired an interior designer, and she knew all my favorite things.

Dropping the bag at the entrance, I spun around in a circle, embracing my freedom, when my phone buzzed.

Xion😁: I see you made it.

Me: Did you really do this for me?

Xion😎: Of course I did.

This place… It's beautiful, X!

Xion😎: It reminded me of how you laugh. Bright, messy, full of color.

I can't believe you did this for me!

Xion😎 I told you. My wife deserves to feel at home somewhere.

You keep saying that word like it's already true.

Xion😎: It is. You already know that, though. I'm just waiting for you to embrace it.

I curled up on the couch, surrounded by light and color, and exhaled. The sound came out half-laugh, half-sigh, like the first breath after surfacing from deep water.

For the first time in a long time, I wasn't surviving. I was living.

CHAPTER TEN

Finally... Free

The sun hadn't even cleared the horizon when my phone started vibrating across the nightstand. Half-asleep, I reached for it, my heart already knowing who it was.

Xion😎🩶.

"Good morning, Mr. Pierce." I smiled, answering the call.

"You sound like sunshine already, Mrs. Pierce." His low laugh filled my belly with butterflies.

"Don't do that."I groaned softly, curling into the sheets.

"Do what?"

"Say my name like it tastes good to you."I groaned softly, curling into the sheets.

"That's because it does. You still in bed?" He

chuckled again, that deep rumble that always made me blush.

"Yes, but only because I was up half the night thinking about you," I teased, half-lie, half-confession.

"Then I'll take the blame for that," he said smoothly. "How's your mother?"

"She's doing better. Your sister-in-law, Dr. Xena, is the truth. She's letting Mama go home today."

"Good. I'll have Xane meet you there later. He'll take care of the arrangements."

"Of course you will." I smiled softly. "You know, it's getting harder and harder to pretend like we're strangers."

"Then stop pretending," he said simply. "You're mine, Harper. Even if you're still catching up to it."

"You really believe that?" I exhaled, voice low.

"I don't believe it. I *know* it. Every time you exhale like that, I feel it."

"You're dangerous." My laugh was quiet, shaky.

"I'm patient," he countered. "There's a difference."

"Patience doesn't usually come with black Amex cards and bodyguards."

"That's just how I show appreciation," he said with a grin in his voice. "You'll learn I'm generous when it comes to the people I love."

The word *love* hung between us like heat. I swallowed, trying not to melt into it.

"Okay, Mr. Pierce," I said softly. "We'll see how generous you really are when you meet my family."

"Oh, I can't wait for that." That may be sooner than you think.

"Oh, really?" I questioned.

We talked for another 10 minutes before he had an alarm go off for a business meeting.

"Well, I guess I should let you go," I say, stretching in the middle of the bed.

"Okay, Mrs. Pierce. Call me when you miss me again." He chuckled out and something in me wanted to kiss this man through the phone.

After our call, I texted my group chat, *Yaya's Angels* 😇, the two women who knew my history, my heartbreak, and still loved me through it all.

Dinner's on me tonight. I will pick you ladies up at 6 PM from Summer's house. Wear something cute. We are celebrating new beginnings

Summer: Oh bitch you know I'm down. ••

Leesa: Oh Lord, here she go again.

Just come, y'all. I'll explain everything in person.

Summer: Bet. I'm going to need the good tequila.

By late morning, I was back at the hospital to check Mama out. When I walked into her room, she was halfway dressed, arguing with the nurse over discharge paperwork.

"I told her I'm fine," Mama said as I entered. "But apparently, they need one more person to sign off."

"That would be me," Xena said, stepping in. She smiled, calm and composed as ever, walking in behind me. "Are you Ready to go home, Mrs. Moore?"

"Been ready," Mama replied. "This place is too quiet. I need to hear Delores yelling at them grand babies, and my own TV."

"Trust me, Ma, you'll get all that and more." I laughed.

"That's good to hear. I just signed off, but there are a few restrictions." Zena said.

"Ah, hell. I knew you were too pretty. Now you're about to put me on adult punishment."

"Not quite." Zena smiled. "You need to take it easy and make sure that you are taking your medications, and Xion has paid for a home companion to come in every day to do your cooking and cleaning so that you can get your rest." My mouth hit the floor.

"Well, I guess I can do that," Mama said, smirking

That's when the door opened and in walked Xane, tall, smooth, with the confidence that ran in the Pierce bloodline.

"Mama, this is Xane," I said. "Xion's twin brother, and Xena's husband."

"It's nice to meet you, Mrs. Moore." He extended his hand.

"Damn," Mama said before she could catch herself. "I mean.. Are you and Xion identical or fraternal twins?" Zena burst out laughing.

"Mama!" I covered my face.

"I see where Harper gets it from. But to answer your question, Xion and I are identical, although I think I am the more handsome of the two." Xane just laughed.

Mama scoffed. "If your brother looks anything like you, Harper better keep him and give me some grand babies." I covered my face in shame as he and Zena laughed.

Within an hour, they had Mama signed out and ready to go. Leo pulled the SUV around, helping her inside while Xane and Zena followed behind in their car.

When we got to the new condo building, Mama stepped out, staring up at the glass tower that glowed in the afternoon sun.

"This is *not* my neighborhood," she said slowly.

"It is now," Xane said, unlocking the front door. "Your new unit is right across the hall from Harper's."

I blinked. "Wait...What?"

"Xion doesn't believe in distance between family, so he made sure that yours was all here in the same area." He smiled.

Mama's mouth fell open. "This man moved me across town and across the hall from my daughter?"

"Not just you," Xane said. "Ms. Delores and her grandkids are in 10C. That way, so you'll never be alone when Harper's traveling."

"That man moves like God and Amazon had a baby." Mama shook her head, tears running down her face.

"That's one way to put it." I laughed so hard my stomach hurt.

When I walked into Mama's new place, it was perfect. There was warm lighting, soft furniture, and photos from her old home, already framed and neatly placed throughout the condo. The fridge was stocked, the pantry full, and a vase of fresh lilies sat on the counter.

"He wanted it to feel like home before you walked in." Xane handed me a set of keys.

"Tell him he succeeded." I bit my lip to keep from smiling too wide.

"I'll tell him," Xane said, glancing at me knowingly. "Or you could call and tell him yourself." I raised an eyebrow, knowing that was Xion's plan all along.

Instead of calling, I had a better idea.

"Mama, come over here so that we can send Xion a thank-you video," I said, walking over to her.

"Girl, I do not have my camera face on. You thank him for me and you!" She winked at me, and I rolled my eyes.

I went to our messages and opened a video message.

"Good afternoon, Mr. Pierce. I wanted to thank you for the amazing surprise you gave my mother and I. You have no idea how much this means to me. Thank you again, Xion. Mrs. Pierce, out." I winked at the end of the video for emphasis and hit send.

Xane and Zena stayed long enough to meet Mrs.

Delores before taking their leave. I went across the hall to my apartment to get ready for my dinner.

By 5:45, I was in Leo's SUV again. I chose a soft, natural makeup look, with curls pinned up, and wore a rose jumpsuit. We arrived at Summer's at six on the dot.

Summer climbed in with a bottle of tequila in her hand. "So... we fighting or celebrating tonight?"

"Both," I said with a grin.

We arrived at a small rooftop restaurant downtown—real cozy, with dim lighting and live jazz humming in the all-glass room.

The waiter had just poured our drinks when Leesa leaned forward.

"Okay, Harper, spill. What's going on? You've been MIA and then drop 'new beginnings' like we supposed to read between the lines."

I sighed, swirling my wine. "I found out Karter and Harley have been sleeping together for months."

"Harley as in your *sister* Harley?" Leesa gasped.

"Why are you acting so surprised? I assumed you knew from our last conversation."

Summer slammed her glass down. "Hold on. You knew and you ain't tell her Leesa? What kind of shit is that?"

The look on Leesa's face was priceless.

"I didn't know shit. I told you everything that I knew and to imply I knew more is fucked up. You think if I had solid proof of her sleeping with your man I would have sat on that fucking information?" She questioned.

"Fuck all that. Did you know or not? Because I knew that the heifer was sneaky! Always smiling too hard at your man like she was auditioning for something. But you are her home girl you supposed to tell her what the fuck you know. "

Leesa's jaw dropped. "If I knew more than I would have told you! Don't you know that?" I think I do. But going forward when you get a hint of something you need to be dialing my phone before you do the research."

"My granny always said, if it smells like shit, it's shit. Maybe not familiar shit but shit nonetheless." We all burst out laughing.

"Have you confronted them yet?" Leesa asked.

"I haven't spoken to Harley but Karter definitely got embarrassed at work when my brother in law handed me the keys to my new condo!" I said sipping my drink victoriously.

"Brother-in-Law?" Summer said, taking my drink from my lips. "Huuhh uh spill bitch."

"So, I'm kinda married, already." I held up my hand showing the ring from Vegas.

Their eyes widened in unison.

"*Married?*" they said together.

"Vegas," I said, a small smile tugging at my lips. "I woke up next to a man named Xion Pierce. We... Well, I thought it was a mistake, but it turns out..."

"Turns out what?" Summer leaned in.

"Turns out he's everything Karter pretended to be. He's smart, funny, patient, protective, and kind."

"So, like, are y'all... actually together now?" Leesa blinked.

Before I could answer, a familiar voice said, "Depends who you ask."

We all turned to see Zena and Xane walking toward our table.

"Harper," Zena greeted, smiling as she kissed my cheek. "We thought we'd join you. Hope that's okay."

"Of course." I motioned for them to sit.

"Is that the man form the bar in Vegas?" Leesa whispered.

"His twin brother." I said quickly.

"Girl, this family fine. They got a factory or something?" Summer whispered.

I nearly spit my drink out laughing.

Xane smiled, nodding to the group. "It's good to meet the ladies from the bachelorette party officially. I was with Xion that night, but left before he made his move. He mentioned you all a few times."

Summer raised a brow. "Oh, he talks about us?"

"Constantly," Xane said. "Especially one in particular."

"Okay, we are not doing this tonight." My cheeks burned.

"Too late. We're doing it." Leesa chuckled.

Dinner flowed with laughter, stories, and more tequila than I planned to drink. I filled them in on the Vegas story, every chaotic, unexpected, magical piece of it — from the accidental vows to Xion's steady patience that somehow made me feel safe.

When I finished, Summer grinned. "So you're telling me you've been planning somebody else's wedding while canceling plans for your own? Girl, that's a story time for your ass."

Everyone laughed — everyone except Zena.

She glanced at her husband, then back at me, a subtle knowing glimmer in her eyes.

"What?" I asked, half-laughing.

She smiled slowly. "Let's just say the CEO whose wedding you've been planning... isn't exactly a stranger."

My laughter froze. "What do you mean?"

Xane raised his glass, his tone teasing but weighted. "You'll find out soon enough. But for now, just know, you've been working for family."

The table went silent for half a heartbeat before Summer blurted out, "Oh, this is about to be *good.*"

I laughed, even as my mind spun. Because somehow, deep down, I already knew,

the story wasn't over.

It was just beginning.

CHAPTER ELEVEN

The Man The Myth The Legend

XION

From the moment I woke up next to Harper Pierce in that Vegas suite, I knew my life had changed. She didn't remember much of that night. Hell, neither did I, not in the way people remember details. But I remembered *her*. The way her laughter echoed over the marble floor. The way she looked at me when the minister said, "Do you?" — like she didn't mean to say yes but couldn't help herself.

I remembered her hands trembling when she signed *Harper M. Pierce* on the certificate, my thumb tracing over the ink as if sealing a promise I didn't even understand yet. It wasn't supposed to be real. But I'm a man who doesn't believe in coincidence. And the more I learned about her, the more I knew that fate had simply stopped playing fair.

At first, I watched from a distance. I wanted her to

have space, to decide for herself if I was a mistake or a miracle. But every message, every call, every stolen moment made it harder to stay away.

She'd text me in the middle of the night sometimes, not even to talk, but just to *be*.

> Mrs. Pierce: Can't sleep.

> Me Either. Missing your snores.

> Mrs. Pierce: I do not snore.

> You sure?

That was our rhythm, her soft confessions met with light banter, and our laughter covering the heat that neither of us wanted to name yet. Every word she typed was gospel to me. I gave her the space to be herself, and in exchange, she granted me trust. While she was learning to find herself again, I was learning about the man who tried to destroy her.

Karter Whitman Peoples.

What kind of fucking name was that? I wasn't even surprised when the search turned up that he had faked his degrees, inflated his work history, and built a resume on forged documents. The deeper I dug, the filthier it got. He didn't just lie, he stole ideas from lower-level associates, marketing them as his own, blackmailed my vendors to make himself look like the prize, and manipulated board members into giving him control he never earned.

He wasn't just a narcissist. He was a fraud. By the time my team finished the investigation, I didn't even have to lift a finger to end him. His own arrogance had written the obituary of his career. All that was left was timing. And timing, I had perfected.

The morning I flew into town, the air felt different, like it was waiting for my arrival. The first stop wasn't my penthouse or the office. It was to meet my mother-in-law.

When I knocked, she called out,

"Door's open, unless you're the bill collector."

I found that funny because she owned the condo, and the utilities were to be paid from my accounts.

Mrs. Moore, Harper's mother, was sitting in her new condo, legs crossed, watching reruns of *Family Matters* like she owned the whole building.

"Not today, ma'am. Just family." I stepped in, grinning.

She turned, and the second she saw me, her eyes

softened in recognition. "So, you're the one my daughter went and accidentally married."

"Guilty," I said, smiling.

"Well Damn," she said, looking me up and down. "I guess she didn't lie. But your brother did. You are clearly the more handsome of the two." She stood pulling me into a hug.

"You're looking good yourself, Mrs. Moore. How are you feeling?" I laughed.

"Better now, I guess I can thank you for that?"

"No thanks needed, ma'am. It's been a pleasure helping." I said honestly.

"Oh, no, sir. It's Mama, not ma'am." I chuckled and nodded.

"Okay, Mama."

"Now, are you here to ask for my permission to marry my baby girl the proper way?"

"I am!" I tell her.

"Well, good. When is the wedding?"

"That's why I am here, the wedding she has been planning has been our wedding."

"So you just know she is going to say yes? Hmmm. Bold. Risky, but bold!"

"Are you taking care of her?" She asked, piercing my soul with her eyes.

"Trying to," I admitted. "But she's a handful."

She smirked. "Good. That means you're doing it right."

We talked for a while about Harper, life, and what love should look like when it's real.

By the time I left, she hugged me tight again like she'd known me her whole life.

"You be good to her," she said softly. "She's been through enough wolves pretending to be men."

"I will," I promised.

The next morning, I set my plan in motion. Leo coordinated everything since he knew her schedule and where her friends stayed. He handled the flowers, breakfast setup, and invitations. I wanted the proposal to be everything she'd dreamed of: sunlight through open windows, laughter in the air, people she loved around her.

When Harper walked into the rooftop café, her hair pulled back and her smile easy, I swear time slowed down. Her mother, Ms. Delores, and the Yaya crew were already seated. Leesa and Summer were grinning like children at Christmas. Even Xane and Zena were there, pretending to act casual.

When she locked eyes with me standing at the table, she froze.

"Xion?"

"Morning, Mrs. Pierce." I smiled, holding her gaze.

"Lawd, I see why she forgot about Karter." Summer fanned herself.

Everyone laughed. Harper's hand trembled as I reached for it.

"You didn't tell me this was breakfast," she said, smiling.

"That's because it's not just breakfast." I dropped to one knee, and reached for her hand.

When I saw my ring on her finger, I stilled, kissed above it like I did in Vegas before looking back up at her. The world went quiet. Even the wind seemed to pause.

"Harper, from the moment you said my name, I've felt like I finally had something worth protecting. You don't need saving, but you deserve peace. You deserve joy. And I want to spend the rest of my life making sure you never forget what both feel like."

Her hand flew to her mouth as tears welled up.

"Will you do me the honor," I continued, pulling the ring from my pocket, "of choosing me again, and being Mrs. Pierce for the rest of this lifetime?"

"Yes. A thousand times, yes." She laughed through her tears.

The table erupted in cheers. Her mother cried. Ms. Delores hollered, "That's right baby!" and waved her napkin in the air.

Then came the moment I'd been waiting for.

I leaned close and whispered, "Harper, the wedding you've been planning..."

"What about it?" She blinked.

"It's ours."

Her lips parted, confusion melting into realization, then joy. "You. You're the CEO. You've been planning this the whole time?"

"I told you," I said softly. "Time was running out."

And just when the world felt perfect, chaos found its cue.

A voice cut through the cheers like a cracked bell.

"Are you serious right now, Harper?"

Every head turned. Harley stood near the entrance, eyes wild, lips tight, jealousy radiating off her like perfume.

"I guess the rumors are true. You were out here

cheating on Karter with his boss. That's low even for you!"

"Who is spreading the rumors? Karter?" Harper said, tone sharp.

"Oh, I know this bitch has lost her mind.. Sorry, Mama," Summer said, standing and removing her earrings.

Harper motioned for Summer to simmer down, and she sat back down but remained at the edge of her seat, removing her shoes.

"You really out here playing wife like you didn't steal my man first?" The crowd went silent.

Harper's smile dropped. "Your *man*? Girl, you mean my ex-fiancé, the same one who was sleeping with his sister-in-law while he was begging me to marry him?"

"Begging you? Girl, he was only marrying you, because I told him no. He thought proposing to you would make me fall in line, but I'm not one to be controlled, unlike you!"

"And yet you are in here talking to me about a man that I don't want, but clearly doesn't want you either. Because why didn't he just crawl back to you when I moved out six days ago?"

"Don't talk to me like that!" Harley snapped. "You always think you're better than me!"

"Because I *am!*" Harper barked back, stepping

forward. "And you proved it the second you traded your soul for a man who doesn't even like himself!"

Summer stood up, fists balled. "Okay, Harley the Harlot, you got about three seconds before I forget I'm a lady!"

"Summer, no!" Leesa grabbed her arm.

Mama Moore rose from her chair, voice firm and commanding.

"Enough!" The room froze.

Even the birds found the nearest power line to perch.

"I raised two daughters, but only one of them remembered how to act like one," she said sharply, eyes locking on Harley.

"Really, Mama, you're going to take her side right now? She has always been your favorite. Daddy was the only one who loved me." She said, starting to tear up.

"Nope. Walk that shit back. I let you use that on me for the last time, last year. And I told your narrow ass then, you will not use your distorted memory of my husband against me. He loved you both equally, and you have made up in your head that he somehow treated you differently, and he didn't." Harley realized that she wasn't going to win.

"Now you can walk out of here with what's left of

your dignity, or you can stay and learn what consequences feel like. Your choice."

Harley looked between them all, face twisted with shame and anger, before storming towards the door.'

"Fuck all of you. Karter has been a better family to me than either of you have been."

Harley turned to leave and I could feel Harper ready to lunge at her, when a shoe flew across the room popping Harley in the back of the head, knocking her wig off. She stumbled forward and we all turned to see Summer standing up holding her other shoe. When Harley turned around to say something Summer beat her to it.

"Keep it moving wench. I got another shoe with your foreheads name on it!" Harley stormed off holding her wig in one hand and her head with the other.

"Lord, I'm too old for this." Mama exhaled, shaking her head.

Then she looked at me and smiled. "Son, let's go get you two married before somebody else tries to steal the spotlight."

CHAPTER TWELVE

The Right Ring

I used to think weddings were all about perfection. The right shade of ivory. The right floral arch. The right playlist that made love sound like a slow-motion movie montage. But standing there in the mirror at the wedding I accidentally planned for myself, I realized I had been aiming too small. Perfection wasn't silence and control; it's laughter and peace.

When I stepped into the garden terrace, the world felt brand new, because I was new. The sun was bright, kissing my skin and warming my soul. The breeze played in the flowers like it had rehearsed with the band. The aisle shimmered with mirrored tiles and cream petals the exact design I had pitched as a dream, not knowing the dream was mine. And at the end of that aisle stood the man I said yes to twice.

Xion looked like he was sculpted out of a promise wearing a black suit, open collar, no tie, like he wanted nothing between us. His eyes softened when he saw me, heat and home wrapped in one look.

Every step I took toward him felt like stepping out of a life that wasn't mine and into one that always had been. Summer sniffled dramatically behind me.

"Lord, that boy is fine." Mama mumbled. I playfully popped her as we made our way down the aisle.

Xane handed tissues out like church ushers at a funeral. I wanted to laugh and cry at the same time. This was happening, and I was going to remember it in the morning.

When I reached him, Xion reached out his hand, ready to guide me up to him.

"You look like God took His time," he whispered.

"And you look like trouble," I whispered back, smiling around my tears.

The officiant cleared his throat like he knew we weren't about to behave.

"We are gathered here to witness the marriage of Harper and Xion Pierce, again..." Everyone chuckled, tension melting like butter.

As he spoke, I didn't look away from Xion once. His thumb stroked my hand slowly, grounding me. His presence felt like safety laced with heat, the kind that stays even after the lights go off.

"I promise," I said, voice trembling but strong, "to never shrink again. To breathe freely. To let you love me without fear."

"And I promise," Xion answered, tone rough with emotion, "to protect your peace like it's my only job. To give you room to grow, even if you grow past me. And to never let time run out on us again." My soul sighed.

That was the vow I didn't know I needed, and when we kissed, it wasn't fireworks; it was a sunrise on true love.

It was steady, warm, and inviting to new beginnings unfolding in real time. Everyone was on their feet, cheering for us.

Mama shouted, "That's my baby!"

"Period!" Summer yelled, while Leesa screamed like she was at Beyoncé's birthday show. And me? I was finally standing in a life that fit. My heart felt wide open and fearless.

I wasn't Ms. Moore. I wasn't Mrs. Peoples. I wasn't an accessory to someone else's ego. I was Mrs.**Harper M. Pierce.**

A woman loved loudly was chosen freely and championed wholly. I wasn't just getting married. I was getting *found*. And this time, the yes was deliberate.

This time, the yes was mine.

The reception felt like a movie scene and seeing my vision come to life was the best. The music pulsed low and warm, glasses clinked, people laughed and danced to as the DJ mixed it up. Mama was on her second glass of champagne telling everyone who would listen, *"That's my baby over there, looking like a million bucks!"*

Summer had already kicked her heels off and was two seconds from auditioning for a Juvenile music video. Leesa found the dessert table and was satisfying her sweet tooth. The make-up artist was crying in the corner because love, apparently, had gotten to her too. While I couldn't stop staring at my husband, who had his hand around my waist. His smile bigger than I had ever pictured as his eyes danced around the room proud, playful, and sure.

Just as the DJ announced the next transition, Xion pulled away with a soft kiss to my temple.

"Don't go far," he whispered.

"Not a chance," I said.

The lights dimmed to a soft amber glow, I watched

as the crowd parted, and the DJ cleared his throat grabbing everyones attention.

"Ladies and gentlemen, please welcome Harper to the floor for her father-daughter dance... with her father-in-love, Mr. Xavier Pierce."

My breath caught. I couldn't believe this was happening. I had forgotten to take the father daughter dance out when I realized it was my wedding.

Xavier stepped forward in a tailored navy suit, eyes gentle, presence commanding, the kind of man who didn't need volume to be heard. He held out his hand to me and I slid mine into his and let him guide me to the center of the dance floor.

The music started.

Ribbon in the Sky by Stevie Wonder, Daddy's favorite song.

I almost lost it right there.

"He would've loved this choice." Xavier smiled warmly.

Tears threatened to fall, catching on my lashes. "It was his favorite."

He nodded. "Xion remembered." His voice softened. "My son pays attention when it matters."

"I miss my dad every day." I swallowed hard.

"I know," he whispered. "A father's presence doesn't end when he leaves this world, it echoes. In the way you love. In the strength you carry. In the soft parts of you that still hope."

"He died when I was twenty-one. The drunk driver didn't even get a scratch. Sometimes I feel like... like life stole something my heart wasn't done with." My chest shook.

Xavier's hand tightened around mine grounding me in the moment.

"Baby girl," he said gently, "I know I can't replace him. I wouldn't dare try. But if you ever need a father to call... a shoulder to lean on... someone to brag to after a big win... or someone to walk you into a room like the world already belongs to you, I'm here." My tears fell, warm and freeing.

"And I will gladly stand in, anytime you want me to."

I leaned my forehead briefly against his shoulder, breathing through the moment.

"Thank you," I whispered. "For choosing me, too."

He chuckled, voice thick with emotion. "Oh no, Harper. *We* are the ones lucky enough that you chose us." He stepped back slightly, eyes shining. "Welcome to the family, darling."

He twirled me slowly, the room spinning into stars, and when he passed me back into Xion's waiting arms at the end, I felt whole in a way I didn't even know I had been broken.

The music shifted to Frankie Beverly & Maze's *Before I Let Go*, and suddenly the dance floor erupted.

Mama grabbed Xion and said, "Let me see if you got rhythm or if I gotta drag my daughter back home!"

He laughed and cut up right with her, matching every step like he'd rehearsed it.

Leesa took the mic from the DJ, impromptu, and delivered a speech that had the whole room crying then laughing then crying again. She said something about "If love don't look like this, I don't want it," followed by "Xion, if you act up, we jumping you, respectfully of course."

"This is the Black love we prayed about!" Summer clinked her glass and announced, before dragging Xena into a wobble line.

The night was a blast, the champagne flowed, cameras flashed, happiness floated around like it was contagious. But while everyone was occupied, Xion pulled me into a corner of the terrace, away from the celebration for a moment.

"You doing okay?" he asked, brushing my lip with his thumb.

"I'm better than okay," I breathed. "I feel amazing, like I'm seeing colors for the first time. I haven't felt like this in a long time!"

"And how do you feel?" He asked leaning in and kissing my neck.

"Free." I gasped as my body reacted to his touch.

He kissed my forehead, then my cheek, then the corner of my mouth. "No," he murmured. "You're finally home."

We re-joined the party, hand-in-hand, as laughter continued echoing off the marble floors and danced under the moonlight.

This wasn't the ending of anything, but the beautiful beginning of everything.

And somewhere inside me, deep in the space that used to ache, was nothing but fullness.

About the Author

Elle De'Von has been captivated by stories for as long as she can remember. After reigniting her passion for reading in 2023, she found herself drawn back to the world of writing, a place that's always felt like home. In 2024, she published her debut novel, Jonesing for Love: Marina's Motif, under the pen name L. Osborne. The months that followed brought personal challenges, but writing remained her anchor and escape.

By September 2025, Elle was ready for a fresh start. Stepping back into the literary scene with a new pen name and a renewed sense of purpose, she's since built a vibrant community that feels like family. Her upcoming novels mark a new chapter—one fueled by resilience, hope, and the magic of second chances. Keep an eye out: you just might spot her latest releases on shelves soon, maybe even in time for B.R.A.E.

ELLE DEVON
Summer's Bloom

Coming January 2026

Coming February 2026

Acknowledgments

This rebrand has been the hardest thing that I've had to do. But with the team of friends that I have built within the book community and those who I know outside of it I have been able to fine my true pen and jump back into writing. I want to thank those people who have been supporting me through it all!

To my alpha, beta, abd arch readers who have been holding me down while I revamped my life. Thank you ladies for being sounding boards and giving honest feedback. It has been amazing working with all of you! And I look forward to your feedback on future projects.

People swear I love drama, but I don't. Drama just loves me because I look good in it. Tonight however, I was trying my hardest to stay far away from chaos. It was suppose to be just Black love poured up like top-shelf wine, and my best friend glowing like God personally hit "increase blessings" on her life. Harper floated past me in that ivory dress looking like a "yes" answered twice. Xion watched her like he intended to keep her smiling for sport. If I cried, mind your business.

I'm on my second glass of champagne, looping the terrace, making sure the vendors hit their cues, call it an occupational standard. When your best friend becomes the hottest wedding planner in the country overnight, you either pitch in or get out the way. So, I pitched in, wearing heels.

"Summer, sit down and be soft," Leesa said, materializing at my elbow with a shrimp skewer and judgment. "You look like you're about to audit the jazz band."

"I *am* about to audit the jazz band," I said, then ate the shrimp. "Also, my feet hurt and these eyelashes are one blink from retirement."

She smirked. "You still fine though."

"Always." I snapped my fingers.

Across the terrace, I spotted Harper's mama two-stepping with Ms. Delores, both of them acting like rhythm owed them rent. A soft Anita Baker track curled around the night, as candles flickering, the whole place dipped in warm gold. Yeah. My girl did that.

I was just deciding if I deserved a tiny, respectful plate of mac and cheese when I felt the air shift. Not the wind. The *room*. Like it inhaled and waited.

He came in from the far side tall, dark skin glowing in the golden lights wearing a navy suit tailored by the Gods, gold frames, beard that looked edged up by an angel. His locs were pulled low, twisted neatly in a barral design. He wasn't moving fast, just with purpose. Like the music kept time for him, not the other way around.

He caught me looking, so I didn't look away. I lifted my chin like: yes, I'm staring. File a complaint.

He stopped in front of me, smile quiet. "You must be Summer."

"Depends who's asking."

"Jaylen Payne." He offered his hand. The first thing I noticed was the size of them, his big palm swallowed my hands but his grip was warm. Not that I was lusting or anything. "Xion's friend."

"Oh, the therapist," I said, letting the word sit with a wink. "Bless your ministry. You take walk-ins? I got some exes that need hands laid on them." He laughed and the baritone shot through my core straight to my G-spot.

"I try not to practice outside the office. But I can make exceptions for emergencies."

"Mm. You diagnosing me already?"

"Not at all." His eyes held mine, steady. "Just observing."

"Observing what?"

"That you guard the people you love like a profession." His voice softened, somehow closer.

"And you forgot where to put that shield when it's just you."

I opened my mouth to clap back, but the truth landed first causing my tongue to stall.

He stood there smirking, he didn't push. Just... waited. Applying pressure to my presence.

I cleared my throat, collected my thoughts. "So you're the soft-spoken type that gets folks to cry in under ten minutes?"

"I'm the type who listens so you don't have to shout." He smiled.

"Cute line."

"Not a line, simply telling you how I operate." he said, liquifying my center.

"Who invited you again?" I asked, pretending I couldn't feel my guard shifting.

"Your best friend's husband," he said. "He told me if I was going to meet family, I should start with the dangerous one."

A laugh busted out of me before I could stop it. "Dangerous?"

"You protect people with your mouth, Summer." His gaze dipped to my mouth and back, not messy, just aware. "It's admirable, but I'm sure you get exhausted!"

"So what, your plan is to tame me?" My heart tripped, just a little.

"Never." He leaned in, close enough for the cologne to say hello. "I don't tame fire. I sit with it, watching the flame dance and warm my hands."

THIS STORY CONTINUES IN SUMMER'S BLOOM COMING TO A SHELF NEAR YOU IN EARLY DECEMBER.

www.ingramcontent.com/pod-product-compliance
Lightning Source LLC
Chambersburg PA
CBHW060328310726
48976CB00007B/2490